HELEN HALL LIB[illegible]
100 WEST WALKER
LEAGUE CITY,TX 77573
DISCARD
W9-BEF-203

A NEW FACE, AN OLD SECRET

Elljay Hallman

PublishAmerica
Baltimore

JAN 11

© 2010 by Elljay Hallman.
All rights reserved. No part of this book may be reproduced, stored in a retrieval system or transmitted in any form or by any means without the prior written permission of the publishers, except by a reviewer who may quote brief passages in a review to be printed in a newspaper, magazine or journal.

First printing

All characters in this book are fictitious, and any resemblance to real persons, living or dead, is coincidental.

PublishAmerica has allowed this work to remain exactly as the author intended, verbatim, without editorial input.

Hardcover 978-1-4512-6401-2
Softcover 978-1-4512-6400-5
PUBLISHED BY PUBLISHAMERICA, LLLP
www.publishamerica.com
Baltimore

Printed in the United States of America

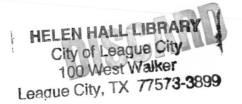

HELEN HALL LIBRARY
City of League City
100 West Walker
League City, TX 77573-3899
DISCARD

This book is dedicated to my husband who always believed I could write.

CHAPTER ONE

"Who do I see about having a face removed?"

"I beg your pardon?" The woman behind the desk lifted heavily mascaraed eyes from her computer and smiled. "Is there some way I can help you?"

"I want to know who's in charge of this art gallery," Jade said with more impatience. Her shaking fingers grazed the edge of her wide-brimmed hat as she reached to remove her dark glasses. "Who has the authority to remove a painting from exhibit?"

"Perhaps I can be of assistance," the receptionist said, slipping from behind the carved mahogany desk. The woman's stylish outfit suited the elegance of these surroundings, Jade noted in momentary distraction. "Was there a painting you wanted to purchase?"

"I don't know what I'll do about it yet," Jade said. "Right now I just want that face taken off the wall."

"I see," the receptionist said, her tone indicative of one with extensive experience in dealing with the public. "Well, why don't we take a look at the painting you have in mind."

The click of high heels on marble floors echoing in Jade's ears like a countdown to doom, she accompanied the other woman down the long corridor.

"Here we are," Jade said, signaling for her to stop in front of a collection of paintings referred to as sensual art. A plaque mounted on the wall indicated that several private collectors had recently consigned this assemblage of oils to the gallery for public sale. "This is the one I mean." She directed her companion's attention to the focal piece of the display and the only unsigned work.

"Oh, yes," the receptionist exclaimed, "this canvas has drawn a great deal of attention. Such intense emotion in the artist's work, art critics have said it compares with the genius of the old masters."

Privately, Jade agreed with the experts' assessment, though, she was sure, not for the same reason. Gathering her courage, she forced her eyes again upon the object of her disquiet.

The woman in the picture was almost naked. Only a man's white shirt shielded her slender body from prying eyes. Unrestricted, the shirttails hung slightly askew, exposing the swell of her full breasts and the delicate twirl of her flat navel before surrendering into modest folds between her thighs. To say the model was beautiful was hardly adequate; any sculptor would have coveted her as his subject.

Her provocative pose added to the subject's attraction. She crouched on one knee beside a shallow stream. A cluster of bright-leafed trees huddled in the background, as if to protect the fragile interloper from the outside world.

Jade's companion uttered an appreciative sigh. "She is remarkable, isn't she?"

"But the face, haven't you looked at the face?" Jade heard the echo of her frustrated rejoinder reverberate along the walls of the corridor.

Recalling her first flush of emotions minutes ago when she'd stumbled upon the the portrait, she pushed her eyes to the part of the woman's anatomy she'd just called to attention. It was fine-boned, almost fragile, yet dramatic in every feature. Especially remarkable were the eyes. There was a profound eloquence about them. Big and round, with just a hint of childlike innocence, they had been colored a green so intense it outstripped the spring grass in the foreground.

The receptionist was correct about one thing: The creator of the piece had captured a multitude of emotions in the face of his subject. The one that touched Jade most was her sadness. No, sadness wasn't quite accurate, she decided now; it was a torment, an agony of shame so devastating it bared its owner's soul as naked as her body.

Though she was still repulsed by the image, as before, Jade felt a simultaneous urge to weep for her.

She turned again to the woman standing next to her. "Now," she said with even greater insistence, "who do I see about having this taken down?"

For seconds, the receptionist studied her with curious scrutiny. Then, "You'll have to talk to Mr. Delancy, our curator, about that," she said. "If you'll come with me, I'll see if he's in."

Back at her desk, she punched a button and, when a deeply male voice came back over the intercom, she explained the situation briefly.

"This lady seems quite insistent," she amended when no reply came back at once.

"Send her in," was the immediate brusque response.

"Right through there." The receptionist pointed toward a door sheathed in highly polished brass.

Jade managed a wisp of a smile. "Thank you," she said.

She sucked in a long breath and marched purposefully toward the brass door. When she stood just outside, she paused to remove the hat she'd worn originally to protect her sensitive skin from Atlanta's late summer sun.

Suddenly impaled by her own reflection, she lingered another moment in front of the shiny metal. Innocent looking for a creature who had inhabited this earth for a quarter of a century, she mused, when a toss of her head loosed a flood of red-gold hair to settle in shimmering billows around a heart-shaped face. Was this an image that belonged on the wall of an art gallery? Wrenching away from her own penetrating gaze, she pumped another restorative breath into her lungs, then lifted her hand to the mirrored surface and knocked.

"Come in," she heard in muffled reply from within.

"Mr. Delancy, I'm here to speak to you about one of the paintings you have on exhibit," she started as soon as she'd crossed the threshold, "the one called,'The Ending Begins'. I want something done about it."

"Close the door." Though the man had not altered his stance in front of the high-arched window, his clipped directive demanded obedience. With his back to her, his tall, shadowed form resembled an artist's silhouette inserted amongst the intense colors of the gardens outside. Another exquisitely carved desk and several black leather chairs barricaded him from her. "Now, what seems to be the problem?" he asked after the door had clamped shut.

"The problem is, that painting is a cruel hoax," Jade continued in a rush. "Obviously, someone who cares only about sensationalizing pain has duped this gallery for his own purposes. And I want it to cease at once. You have to take down that painting!"

Caught up in the urgency of her plea, she was less than prepared when the man turned toward her and looked straight into her face. She detected a fleeting reaction of disbelief before he resumed his piercing scrutiny.

Meanwhile, she had commenced her own assessment. His dark suit covered a physique so well put together she felt unsafe even perusing it. His skin, bronzed and unblemished, could scarcely have weathered more than thirty Georgia summers. The fact that no gray had yet crept into his generous allotment of chestnut hair reinforced her conjecture.

His finely chiseled features likely attracted women like connoisseurs to a fine work of art. But his current visitor had acquired some measure of immunity to superficial attraction during the past few months. No question, she felt the effect of him; even now a flush of heat in her nether regions and a simultaneous shudder contradicted the perfect comfort of the room. Yet something in the set of the man's features at once restored her feeling of cautious restraint. Emanating a potency as lethal as the elderberry wine concocted by the notorious Brewster sisters, those dark eyes, also, harbored an unresolved anger. And the way he looked at her; she felt a sudden contraction of her muscles, as if she'd touched cold stone.

He hadn't said anything in response to her demand. His intense scrutiny continued to consume every part of her, like an astronaut bound for some distant universe gorging his senses with the physical form of an earth woman.

"Tell me who you are." Again she heard more command than request in his tone.

"I'm looking for Cain Delancy," she said, determined not to allow his fascination- -or hers—to confuse the purpose of her visit. "If you're not the man in charge of this art gallery, perhaps you'd be good enough to direct me to him."

"You have an extraordinary face," he said. "Especially those eyes of yours."

So, when he looked at her, he saw an "extraordinary" face, Jade mused. Accustomed to hearing "pretty" or even "beautiful" in reference to her features, nevertheless, she'd seldom been swayed by vanity in her responses. Quite the contrary, more than once she'd had occasion to berate the male distraction with her winsome features. And certainly, if this man meant to throw off her defenses with a compliment, he'd just lost his edge.

"I could say the same about yours," she returned. Like a poison you'd been warned to avoid, but can't seem to wean yourself away from, she wasn't rude enough to add out loud.

She could have sworn he stifled a grin, if the curling of one corner of his mouth constituted a smile.

"I'm sure you have a busy schedule," she said with added firmness. "And my business is very personal, as you've probably guessed. So, if you'll just tell me where I can find Mr. Delancy—"

"Won't you sit down." Once again what might have been a simple voicing of good manners sounded more like a command than a courtesy.

"As I've explained, my business is with Mr. Del—"

"I'm Cain Delancy," he said. "Now, sit down…please." The final word came out hesitantly, as if foreign to his lips.

Jade nodded and, gathering the folds of her sheer summer frock, glided lightly into the nearest chair.

"Do you own this gallery?" she solicited after he'd settled himself behind the massive desk.

He shrugged. "Cy and Leona own it—officially. We have a kind of—partnership."

"Cy and Leona? Would they be family, your brother and sister perhaps?"

That odd hint of a smile appeared again. "I have a brother somewhere but he has no interest in this gallery. No, Cy and Leona are my parents—in a manner of speaking. And now that I've introduced myself, would you mind telling me who I've been conversing with these past few minutes."

"Oh, I'm Jade, Jade Hartman." A pinch of sadness for what sounded like a peculiar family relationship blended with embarrassment in her reply.

"Jade Hartman…" He stroked her name in a tone turned to pure silk. Likewise, his gaze had become a caress of her features, ultimately pausing to compare the jade locket she wore to eyes that were the same mysterious shade of green. "I might have guessed," he murmured so low she barely heard.

His accounting of her features continued until it was almost an intimate touching. When so much about his demeanor struck a discordant note in her brain, why, at the same time, did she feel her emotions being plucked with the skill of a prodigy to the strings of a Stradivarius?

Feeling her strength of purpose ebbing away, she pushed her senses to remember her errand here.

"Maybe I should apologize for barging into your office, Mr. Delancy," she said. "I don't usually behave so impulsively. But you have to understand, I hadn't expected to find myself offered up for public view like that."

One dark eyebrow arched. "Do you think the artist's portrayal of his subject is obscene?" he asked.

At least he hadn't tried to pretend he didn't recognize the face as hers. "More than that—it strips me of my dignity, my honor."

His hawk-like gaze gave way temporarily to an oddly startled look. "My dear girl," he wrapped his tongue around the casual familiarity, "how can you take offense at something so beautiful?"

"You may think it's beautiful," she said, "but it makes me feel as if some stranger had violated my person, then stripped it naked for everyone to gawk at.

"My work is with languages, Mr. Delancy," she went on before he could comment. "I don't know any artists and I've never granted anyone, professional or otherwise, permission to paint my portrait. I would never pose like that, in any case. So this likeness of me had to have been distorted to its present condition by some person without scruples. Since I'm certainly not flattered by such a presumptuous act, I have to insist you remove it from exhibit."

"I'm afraid I can't do that," he said.

"Then, please call your parents and explain the situation so they can authorize you to take it down."

"I can't do that, either," he said with added bluntness.

Two months ago, such a rebuke might have moved her to tears. Already she felt a rush of moisture at the back of her eyelids. Intending only to shield her from life's cruelties, instead, her mother had sent her forth a knight without armor into a world filled with dragons. Nevertheless, the tortures she'd been subjected to during the past several months had forced stouter stuff into her defenses. They must hold fast against her current tormentor.

"Mr. Delancy," she said, swallowing to control her tone, "maybe here in your world you're accustomed to doing anything you please. But don't let my appearance fool you. I won't permit you to use me to further your own interests. I'm acquainted with a few lawyers back in Washington, D.C. Perhaps it would be better if I ask one of them to continue this matter with you."

She wondered if he saw in her features the force of strength it had taken to make that valiant speech. She recalled the reaction of another man she'd threatened recently with legal action. And the consequences!

Though grace followed her movements like a placid companion, nevertheless, she instilled determination into her steps as she exited the chair and turned toward the door.

The words, "I might consider letting you have the painting," stopped her in midstride.

Her hand already on the doorknob, Jade twisted her head and stared at the man who, only moments ago, had set himself against her with such obstinate disregard. "I beg your pardon? What did you say?"

"I said I might consider letting you have the painting."

"Is this some kind of joke, Mr. Delancy?" Her hand dropped from the doorknob and she turned to face him again. "Since you seemed so adamant before, I have to think you value that painting more than my feelings. So, why the sudden change of heart?"

"It has nothing to do with heart, Miss Hartman." He appeared wryly amused at the play on words. "It's simply a matter of exchange of values."

"Exchange of values? Aside from money, what could I possibly offer that you might accept in payment for what is obviously a valuable piece of art?" At once, she recoiled at the implication she'd inadvertently inserted into her retort.

"Information," she heard him say.

"I don't understand."

"What I want from you, Miss Hartman, is information," he said. "I want you to tell me who painted it."

CHAPTER TWO

"This *is* a joke," Jade said, hardly believing the gall of Cain Delancy. "And a very sick one, at that."

"Not at all," he said. "I'm anxious to gain information about the author of that painting. I placed it with the rest of the exhibit because it suited my purpose."

Thinking she'd witnessed the extent of his conceit, nevertheless, she was almost confounded by this blatant declaration. "You-you think I can tell you who's responsible for that painting? Haven't I just explained that I've never given anyone permission to paint my portrait?"

"The woman in that painting isn't you, as you must know, Miss Hartman."

"But I don't know," she said, confused again. "And you haven't denied…How can you be certain it's not a painting of me?"

"Because, if my guess about your age is correct, that canvas was painted at least five years before you were born."

This latest scrap of information prompted Jade to conduct a frantic search of her memory. If what Cain Delancy had said was true, then who might the woman in the painting be? Among the few pictures her mother had kept of herself and family members, she couldn't recall anyone whose features might have mirrored her own thirty years ago. Could this painting simply be dismissed as an odd coincidence? Or had Fate taken a hand in her public humiliation?

"Why didn't you tell me that right away?" she demanded aloud. "Instead of letting me carry on like a mad woman these past few minutes?"

"Frankly," he said without a trace of apology, "I was interested in what you might unwittingly tell me."

"Oh, I see." Rage again rooted out disbelief for control of her emotions. "Well, I'm sorry to disappoint you, Mr. Delancy, but I don't know a thing that might help you."

"Perhaps you know more than you think you do," he said.

"I don't know *anything*," she reiterated, "except that that portrait looks like me and I view it as a personal slander."

Again one dark eyebrow lifted. "Surely, you've misinterpreted what you saw," he said. Like a vampire who must satisfy his peculiar hunger to continue, his gaze fed upon the lines of her body. "I assure you I intended to communicate sensuality in that exhibit, not sex."

"I would never consent to display my figure like that," she said, privately congratulating herself for winning back a semblance of calm to her voice. "But it's not the body's near undress in the painting that offends me most."

He appeared more puzzled than ever. "Then, what is it about the subject that has you so upset?"

Jade couldn't believe he really didn't know. However, "You told me a minute ago that I have extraordinary eyes," she said by way of clarification.

"Yes. But 'expressive' might have been a more accurate term."

"Have you ever looked closely at the eyes of the woman in that portrait?"

"Yes, I think I have."

"An yet you can't see why I don't want the painting put up so people can stare at it? I can understand why you purchased it, but—"

"I'm not following you," he cut in. "There's nothing about any of the features that I can see to make you feel ashamed."

A discreet skirting of the truth wouldn't satisfy him, she realized. He expected her to spell it out—in bold, hard letters.

Breathing out a long sigh, "Mr. Delancy," she said, "if you'd ever hurt so much you didn't know whether you could live with the pain, wouldn't you mind if an image of what you'd been feeling showed up in a public place?"

She saw her latest volley carried more impact than anything she'd thrown at him so far. For long seconds, he stared at her.

"Since that isn't you in the painting, Miss Hartman," he said finally, "how can it matter?"

With that, Jade accepted that continuing this conversation was futile. Cain Delancy was a hard man. Short of revealing the brutal turns her life had taken during recent months, she had no hope of making him understand. And even after he learned the whole story, would he care? So far, her distress hadn't moved him. Once again she turned, determined this time to complete her exit.

Only one thing would have stopped her: "I'll give the order to take down the painting at once."

It did. "And you'll let me buy it from you?"

"Why don't we have dinner together this evening so we can discuss it," he sidestepped.

Jade struggled to balance her perception. Except for that one fateful venture, indulgence of her sexual longings had barely progressed beyond soda shop hand holding.

According to her senses' own clamorous warnings, this man possessed a virility more powerful than that of the man whose maleness had seduced a foolish innocent once before. Laying her heart open that time had invited consequences which might have devastated the spirit of even the most worldly woman. If she'd gained any wisdom from her tragic experience, it was to stay away from men like Cain Delancy.

Still, he'd made a gesture toward concession; he'd promised to remove that painting from public view. Perhaps a few hours with him in a social atmosphere was worth the risk. She might persuade him to accept a reasonable purchase price for the portrait.

"I guess dinner would be all right," she said. "I'll have to pick up my bags at the hotel first, though, and make arrangements for a room for another night. I'm only here in Atlanta for a short vacation, and I hadn't meant to stay over another day. Can I meet you somewhere later?"

"Why don't I take care of all that for you," was his immediate counter. "Since I've been the cause of you delaying your departure, allow me to make arrangements for your hotel. Where are you staying?"

"The Empire, but—"

"Of course. I know it well," he said, breaking into her attempt at protest. And before she could offer up any reasons for objecting, he lifted the phone and dialed a number. "Yes, Cain Delancy here," he said to someone at the other end and, at once, began to issue instructions concerning her accommodations.

"There, you're all taken care of," he pronounced as he hung up the phone. "The manager at the Empire assures me he'll have another room prepared for you, and your bags should be transferred to it by the time you return. Would you like me to go with you to make sure everything's satisfactory? I could drive you—"

"Thank you, no" she said, finally managing to cut him off. A quick review of the progression of events told her to fall back quickly and reconnoiter. This man played a fast and skillful game, and she'd lost track of where she stood with him. "I have a rental car and I'm perfectly capable of handling things from here on."

He backed off this time. "Good. Then, I'll call for you at eight o'clock."

Before she'd hardly become aware of his actions, he moved from behind the desk and stood over her. The polished finesse of this man continued to astound when she found herself smoothly ushered from her chair and out of his office. Regardless of her attempts to force his compliance to her demands, she realized, Cain Delancy had remained in control of the situation from the time she'd entered his office. Not only had he placated her indignation about the painting, but he'd as much as blackmailed her into a social engagement. How else was he manipulating her, she wondered with renewed uneasiness.

"Just for the record," she felt compelled to inquire after he'd punched the elevator button, "how do I know you'll really remove that painting from exhibit?"

Jade watched his polite smile fade into a look of sober earnestness. "I don't lie to people, Miss Hartman," he said. "And I don't forgive easily anyone who does. But." he added, the return of his smile removing some of the edge from his harsh pronouncement, "you can see for yourself tomorrow."

Before she could tell him she didn't plan to be around tomorrow, the doors to the elevator closed. "Who was that woman?"

Rena Taval had followed Cain back into his office carrying several letters which required his signature. He'd often commended himself for the choice he'd made when he hired Rena. Adept with people, as well as physically attractive, she had proved a valuable asset to the gallery during the year she'd worked here. She had executed her duties with skill as impeccable as her appearance.

Except for his strict rule against intimate relationships with employees, Cain might have had a fling with Rena by now. Oddly, though, as he looked at her now, he could see no attraction in her imposed beauty to compare with the unaggressive elegance of the woman who'd just left.

"Our visitor's name is Jade Hartman," he informed her when he handed back the signed papers.

"I barely caught a glimpse of her features," Rena commented, "but I could swear she looked like—"

"I know who she looks like," Cain interrupted. "But she's not."

"Then, what was she doing here?" Rena asked

"That's something I'm going to find out," he said musingly. "Don't let anyone disturb me for the next few minutes, Rena," he added, his businesslike tone back in command. "I have a phone call to make."

Alone in his office, Cain wrestled with an impatience that bordered on desperation. Seeing the face in a thirty-year-old painting replicated in a young woman had really shaken him. Even as he'd let Jade Hartman go just now, he'd felt a compelling urge to reach out and pull her back for fear he might never see her again.

"Get hold of yourself, man," he counseled aloud, "she's only a woman. But maybe a very valuable one."

He lifted the phone and punched in the number of the Larkins' import business. Impatient again at having to wait while her secretary paged Leona, who apparently was somewhere out on the showroom floor, he paced back and forth, combing his fingers carelessly through his thick auburn hair.

"Leona, hello," he spoke up when he heard the familiar voice at the other end of the line, "I'm calling to let you know I'm bringing a guest for dinner this evening…Yes, it's a woman…No, it's no one you've met before."

So like Leona, he thought, always reacting to any change with unruffled acceptance. Very few things flustered her. He'd seen her self-control disintegrate once, however, when he'd brought out that stack of old canvases he'd discovered in a storage room at the gallery. That time, he'd seen her practiced assurance shatter like candy glass.

"I can't wait for you meet this woman, Leona," he said aloud. His lips curled into a derisive smirk. "I think you'll find her very interesting."

Cain dropped the receiver into its cradle. A pang of remorse instantly sobered his features. Perhaps he shouldn't do this. Cy and Leona had treated him well enough, and they'd provided him with some semblance of a family during most of his life.

"No, damn it!" he gritted in self-vindication. "I can't get them to tell me anything about myself any other way. Somebody else has to know where I came from. And maybe I've just stumbled on that very person."

As the engine of her rental car purred to life, Jade wondered again whether she'd made the right decision about accepting a dinner invitation from Cain Delancy. But it was done. Now what she had to concentrate on was a stronger line of defense against the powers of this cunning adversary.

In minutes, Jade had maneuvered out of the parking area and onto the service road leading to the freeway. She'd told Mr. Delancy that she knew her way around Atlanta. She hadn't revealed to him that it was her home town. She couldn't actually remember living here, but her birth certificate listed it as her birthplace. A few years ago after she'd decided to re-establish citizenship in the country of her origin, she'd come back here hoping she might find a job that suited her talents. However, when nothing presented itself immediately, she'd expanded her search and eventually accepted a position as an interpreter for the State Department in Washington, D.C.

Life in Washington had proved rewarding enough—that is, until her new boss, Bonn Corbett, had spoiled it. What had transpired between them had soured her taste for life in the nation's capital and almost destroyed her personally.

Once again, Atlanta had been the only place she could run to that felt like home. Her sojourn here had furnished her with time to collect herself and mull over a job offer at the French embassy in New York. She'd enjoyed an uneventful respite until this afternoon's dilemma had cropped up.

Well, she would neutralize the situation tonight. Whatever Cain Delancy's agenda might be, it had nothing to do with her. As soon as she was certain that picture was gone, she would be, too.

A discreet signpost indicated The Golden Empire Hotel just ahead. It was one of those beautiful old red brick hotels which paid homage to the elegant style of ante-bellum architecture. Flawlessly manicured lawns accented by lush beds of petunias and periwinkles surrounded the white-columned structure, reminding guests that graciousness had not disappeared along with the old South.

"We've transferred your luggage to Suite 402, Miss Hartman," the desk clerk informed Jade when she stopped at the front desk to complete arrangements for her night's lodgings.

"But my old room was fine," she protested, thinking about the added cost of a suite.

"Already booked, I'm afraid," the clerk replied.

"Mr. Delancy requested that we take good care of you," a voice from behind her announced. "George Hedley, hotel manager, at your service, Miss Hartman," he said when she turned around. The thin man at her elbow was so impeccably groomed his clothing showed so sign of his ever having sat in them. He acknowledged her with a slight bow, then continued, "It's our pleasure to accommodate you. Mr. Delancy is one of our most valued customers. We do our best to satisfy all his family's clients." The precise features of the little man beamed with pride. "Please enjoy your suite and let us know if there's anything else we can do to make your stay more comfortable."

"Uh-thank you, Mr. Hedley," Jade said, silently weighing whether she should present any further objection. She was keenly aware of the manager's reserved scrutiny.

How many other female "clients" had Mr. Delancy sent to him on short notice? "There is one thing," she resumed aloud, "Could you arrange for a garment to be pressed right away for me?"

"Of course." With fastidious swiftness, Mr. Hedley beckoned for a bellboy.

"Attend to this lady, Martin," he instructed the young man. "She'll also have some pressing for you to take care of, I believe." The task delegated, the manager provided Jade with a properly ingratiating smile. "Now, if there's anything else, Miss Hartman, please don't hesitate to ask."

Obvious he assumed he'd fulfilled his duties, he issued her another slight bow and flitted away, like a hummingbird with other flowers to attend to.

"So this is how you 'take care' of your clients, Mr. Delancy," Jade whispered when the bellboy ushered her into a magnificently appointed suite. She'd hardly been visible to the management during her previous stay. Now because of Cain Delancy's "arrangements," she rated this? Well, it was only for one night. And she hadn't properly celebrated her birthday. Why not indulge herself with a luxury suite for one night?

"This is the dress I need pressed," she had, handing the garment to the bellboy along with his tip.

Pampered by her soak in a tub the size of a wading pool, Jade felt sufficiently restored. She'd barely dried off when she heard the bellboy's knock. Mr. Hedley inspired efficiency in his staff, she credited when she reached to accept her freshly pressed cocktail dress.

An hour later, she'd finished her toilette and was ready to shed her silk dressing gown and slip into the delicate garment she'd had prepared to wear this evening. The mint green fabric glided smoothly over her body, its slim lines falling easily into place around the curves of her figure. Critiquing her appearance before the mirror, she decided one piece of jewelry, a gold necklace made up of a dozen delicate chains secured at either end, furnished just the right complement to the simple elegance of her frock.

Her hair required some additional thought. What style would show her escort she was offering no more than a few hours of cordial conversation to repay his courtesy?

When after several attempts to tightly confine her thick locks in a French twist, she decided to permit a few wispy curls to escape. Her flawless complexion required little more than a few touches of cheek blush and lip gloss and she was done.

"Not too bad," she pronounced to the flattering image in the mirror. However, for a woman who didn't generally dwell on her appearance, she had to admit she'd just gone to a great deal of trouble.

"You look cool enough to sip on a summer day." That was the immediate assessment offered by the man who appeared at her door minutes later. His eyes supped her up like a man thirsty for refreshment. She didn't respond aloud but her mind certainly had its say. His white dinner jacket and tailored slacks fit just snugly enough to accentuate his strongly masculine physique. That earlier dark image seemingly left behind, his features glowed with rakish good looks and potent male charm.

"I hope I'm dressed for whatever you had in mind for the evening, Mr. Delancy." she said, risking a tentative smile.

"You're perfect for what I have in mind," he said with so much soberness it puzzled her. "And really, Miss Hartman, I'm only thirty-two," he said, back to his teasing lightness, "not quite in my dotage yet. I leave formality behind at the gallery. How about we make it Cain and Jade from now on?"

"I don't—all right," she conceded, forfeiting some of her caution. "I guess we could make it Cain and Jade—for this evening."

He seemed to find her hesitation somewhat amusing, but he didn't voice any rebuttal. Instead, "Shall we?" he said and held out his arm to escort her toward the elevator.

"That one's mine," he said, nodding toward the silver Lincoln SUV parked at the curb. The doorman rushed to open the passenger door as Cain led her through the hotel's front exit. Her escort was as skilled behind the wheel as he was with verbal manipulation, Jade noted when he guided the SUV deftly into evening traffic. Acutely aware of their closeness inside the vehicle, Jade maintained a silent vigil beside her companion. She was fluent in a dozen languages and even decently competent in signing; nevertheless, she hesitated to initiate any kind of social exchange with this sexually intimidating man.

It was impossible not to look at him, though. The outer signs of his manhood, strong hands gripping the steering wheel with skillful ease, hard thigh muscles straining against his trousers; they were every bit as potent as passionate dialogue. When her eyes strayed to the slight pucker below his belt, she snatched her gaze in another direction.

"Where are we going?" she spoke up with sudden awareness that they had moved out of the commercial areas of downtown Atlanta.

Without answering at once, instead, Cain pulled the Lincoln off the main thoroughfare and onto a forest-enveloped side road.

"Cain?" she prompted. "What's going on? This looks like a residential area."

"You'll see in a minute," he answered finally. "The house is just up ahead."

"Whose house?"

"It belongs to Cy and Leona Larkin."

As if his revelation had been its cue, a two-story residence of maroon brick presented itself from behind the latest grove of trees. A masterpiece of Southern architecture, Jade had to admit. Behind its white-painted columns, lofty verandas and well-cared-for lawns, she could almost envision Scarlett O'Hara sweeping down a grand staircase in her voluminous satin skirts. But those days were long buried amid war and destruction. And houses like these now sheltered the gentry of the new South.

"It's beautiful," she commented, "but it's not what I expected. I thought you were taking me to a restaurant for dinner."

"Change of plans," Cain dismissed with the same stubborn absence of apology which had annoyed her earlier today. "I thought you might find it a more unique experience to have dinner here."

"You might have—" she started, then, "Won't your parents mind if you just drop in with an unannounced guest?" she finished instead.

"Not at all. In any case, I told them I might bring you to dinner with me. I'm sure they'll find you very interesting." If he'd meant his smile to reassure her, he'd missed on that one.

Cain had an unusual range of definitions for the word "interesting," Jade decided minutes later when his parents greeted them at the front door. At the sight of her, the older couple grabbed for one another, like earthquake victims seeking something solid to hold to when everything around them begins to tremble and shatter.

"Jade, these are my parents, Cy and Leona Larkin," Cain said, emphasizing the different last name. Nothing in his expression showed he'd reacted to his family's disquiet at seeing her. However, he turned watchful as he announced, "Cy, Leona, I want you to meet Miss Jade Hartman."

"I'm sorry if I startled you," Jade said. Empathy with the Larkins furnished her with enough courage to cast an admonishing glance at Cain. "I'm guessing your son hasn't told you about my resemblance to the portrait in your gallery."

"No-o, Cain didn't mention anything about it." Leona Larkin let go of her husband's hand and extended the freed appendage to Jade. "What an odd coincidence, my dear," she said, a slight tremor still edging her voice. "You're welcome here, of course," she hastened to amend. She darted a cautious glance at her son. "We can't wait to hear how the two of you met.

"Why don't we move out to the veranda," she said before anyone could furnish a reply. "Cy and I were just about to have a little something to drink before dinner."

"This way, Jade," Cain said. With the same subtle touch he'd used this afternoon to effect his wishes, her escort placed his hand at the small of her back and guided her along the long halls that apparently led to a rear veranda.

She would never have taken the Larkins for Cain's relatives, she mused as they walked along behind the older couple. Although his stocky physique bulged around the middle these days, clearly, Cy Larkin had once possessed the heavy-muscled build of a wrestler. Leona was short like her husband and, despite the careful tailoring of her cocktail dress, full-figured plumpness dominated her figure. Fair skin and light hair was another trait the couple had in common. Leona probably spent a good deal of time at the hairdresser's to achieve her stylish coiffure, but Cy's thinning crew cut might have been the work of any sidewalk barbershop.

Their physical differences alone would have prompted Jade to question their blood relation to Cain. But the manner of his introduction seemed intended to reaffirm his peculiar reference to them earlier today.

"How kind of you to invite me into your home on such short notice," Jade said when Leona handed her the glass of white wine she'd requested. Her escort's slight intimacy still disturbing her senses, she struggled to hold her voice steady. However, the need to clarify her presence coaxed her to continue. "Actually, I'd never intended to impose on your hospitality. I just wanted to make some kind of arrangement to buy the painting I mentioned. You see, I'm in town on a short vacation and I spotted it during my visit to your gallery this afternoon."

"Oh, I see." Leona exchanged another glance with her husband, and they both seemed to relax a little. "Well, you'll have to work that out with Cain, of course. The gallery is strictly his domain. His father and I concentrate on the import business. Ah." she amended, shifting her gaze toward the door, "there's Nellie to announce dinner. Shall we go inside?"

As the evening continued, the older couple seemed to relax even more. Their questions to Jade about her work and her hobbies hinted at no deeper motive than a desire to become better acquainted. Responding to this unaffected behavior, she felt her own tension subside. With a wealth of stories to draw from concerning personalities she'd encountered at the State Department, she soon had her dinner companions thoroughly entertained.

"The worst exchange I've ever witnessed took place only recently," she confided. I was translating at a meeting between one of our diplomats and a Middle Eastern gentleman. Our representative, I'm sorry to say, was a man whose influence had secured his position much too long. He was only attending this meeting because no one else was available. He had become hard of hearing, which compounded the difficulties. The Middle Eastern representative was well known for his impatience."

"It must be difficult to convey information precisely under such strained circumstances," Leona said with interest. "I've always wondered how translators do it."

"Usually, I concentrate on making accurate translations so the speakers don't bother me. But this time I had to repeat myself over and over because the deaf man said he didn't understand." She chuckled. "Finally, the Middle Eastern man shouted a curse mentioning the part of the anatomy where the poor old guy must have his head. I told him I wouldn't repeat that in any language, and the two of them could just sit and stare at one another if they couldn't behave. Well, neither man had any trouble understanding that."

Cy and Leona laughed along with Jade. Cain seemed to enjoy the conversation; however, other than an occasional nod or half-smile, he appeared content to sit quietly and observe while his parents enticed their guest into revelations about herself.

As dinner ended, the Larkins grew more silent, also. After finishing his coffee, Cy leaned over and spoke a few words for Leona's ears only, then rose abruptly from his chair.

"I hope you'll excuse me," he said, addressing his petition to Jade. "I need to speak to Cain for a few minutes before he leaves—about a business matter."

Puzzled at this breach of etiquette from a host who had been nothing but gracious, nevertheless, Jade nodded. "Of course, I understand."

She caught an odd look of triumph in Cain's eyes before he, too, excused himself and followed his father out of the room. In spite of her hostess's attempts to cover with light conversation, during the next several minutes, Jade overheard the sounds of a heated argument from a nearby room. It broke off suddenly and, a minute later, Cain reappeared alone. His countenance now bore the same look of barely contained anger she'd noticed during their first meeting.

"Cy wants you in the office right away," he said to Leona.

"But, our guest—" his mother started.

"Jade will be fine with me." Cain's clipped interruptions had a way of sounding like orders, Jade noted, remembering her own earlier experience.

Whether it was his reply or his stony expression that stopped her, in any case, Leona put forth no further protest. However, Jade saw a look of pain pass across her features before she forced it away with a smile.

"Jade, my dear, do come back to see us again," she said to their guest. The deliberate set of her features notwithstanding, her invitation sounded genuine.

"I will if I can," Jade said, graciously omitting her wish that she might never have to deal with this family again. "Thank you for your hospitality, Mrs. Larkin."

When his mother rose to leave the veranda, Cain offered nothing more than a nominal gesture of good manners to acknowledge her exit.

"So, Jade, let's see if we can find a better place to talk." The tone of his remark indicated an effort to curb its brusqueness. Before she could decide whether going with him was a good idea, he'd urged her from her chair and ushered her through another side door. "Here, this will do," he said minutes later when they arrived at a small parlor at the opposite end of the house.

Cain's recent behavior a clear signal, Jade conceded that their social evening was at an end and accepted the seat he offered. Her host shed his dinner jacket and tossed it onto the back of the overstuffed chair opposite her. But he didn't sit. Instead, he propped his hips against the chair's arm and scissored one long leg across the other. All too aware that her eyes, unguarded, would give away her body's response when his hard thigh muscles squeezed against the light fabric of his trousers, Jade quickly looked away. Why, she had to wonder, when she wasn't sure whether she liked or trusted him, was this man able to seduce her with his every motion?

He, on the other hand, seemed to be having no trouble focusing on his purpose.

"Now," he said, "about that information you were going to share with me about the painting."

His abrupt prompting jarred her mind's erotic wanderings to an untidy halt. "I told you," she said with equal abruptness, "I don't know anything that could interest you. Can't we get away from that subject? The only reason I came here tonight was to—"

"You probably know a great deal that I would find interesting," he persisted, interrupting her solicitation. "Why don't we start by—?"

"Mr. Delancy," she imposed, swapping interruptions. When one dark brow lifted in that familiar arch, "All right, Cain," she corrected, "anyway, I'd really prefer that you don't continue with this line of thought any longer. It can get us nowhere, I assure you, and I can't afford to spend any more time with this," she hurried on before he could reverse control again. "I have to make a decision about a new job. Can't we concentrate on working out some arrangement for my purchase of the painting?"

He didn't answer her directly; rather, he posed what seemed an odd question. "What would you do with the painting if you owned it?"

She attempted to shrug off the query. "What I do with it after I purchase it shouldn't matter to you. All I want is for you to set a price so we can get on with this transaction. I have to catch a plane back to Washington in the morning."

Another surge of that dormant anger flared and briefly threatened to spew in her direction. In a matter of seconds, however, it bubbled back down and he capped it off.

"Very well, Jade," he said in a voice that had become ominously quiet, "if that's the way you want it. To date, I've had three offers for that canvas. The highest bid was for one hundred thousand dollars."

His revelation accomplished the effect he'd obviously intended. She felt her body constrict with astonishment. Her senses anticipating an angry retort moments ago, she did manage to pull down her eyelids before her telling eyes gave her away. Temporarily shielded, she seized the opportunity to make a quick decision.

"All right, if that's the price," she bluffed. "I'll have a certified check ready for you as soon as the bank opens on Monday morning."

"The painting's not for sale!" The pronouncement came out of his mouth with such a spurt of unleashed fury that Jade had no time to guard her eyes. Her eyelids shot open full with unconcealed shock. The next instant, jade green orbs collided head on with a pair almost pitch black with rage.

Too late she recognized the foolishness of her ploy. An amateur who'd taken the offensive in a battle of wits with a man who played his game with a master's skill, she'd defeated her own cause. This time when she jerked down her eyelids, it was to prevent Cain from seeing her pain in a dramatic spill of tears. Raw emotion shoved her from her chair. Then desperation took over, guiding her in the only option left—escape.

Through a watery blur, somehow, she managed to find her way to French doors leading to another veranda. Fumbling blindly with the latch, a second later she felt the evening breeze touch a cooling hand to the tears scalding her cheeks.

In the next second, she felt another caress, this time from gentle hands wrapping around her shoulders like a delicately woven shawl.

"Jade," she heard whispered as she was gently turned around. Far from the harsh ultimatum grated through those same lips only moments ago, Cain's utterance of her name was, itself, a caress.

Unable to halt her reaction, she lifted her eyes to seek out the dark mystery in his. The impulsive response gave her no time to hide feelings washed crystal clear by her tears.

"Jade?" Hearing him speak her name again, she detected a genuine urgency in his voice. Then, with his eyes still fixed on hers, he moved his mouth closer. A hair's breadth before all their former harshness disappeared from his eyes, she discerned his purpose.

The kiss caressed her lips with such sensual softness, she was trapped before she could think to jerk her head away. Every reasonable thought pushed aside, she let her eyelids drop and allowed her senses to fill up with him. The cautions of her rational mind continued unheard as she flattened her palms against the warm hardness of his chest.

That same wise voice tried vainly to warn her that her own lips hadn't remained passive during his violation. An accomplice to her own seduction, she thrilled with a kind of euphoria she hardly understood. Nothing in her meager repertoire of experience had prepared her for the turmoil within. Raw desire struggled to unleash itself, jerking her senses every which way. A ravishing need racked her body to embrace everything this man offered—and more.

A matchstick in the wind to the whims of passion, she barely noticed the change in her seducer. Somehow, his gentle exploration had evolved into obtrusive stalking, then unmitigated invasion. Pillaging lips pried hers apart and a coarser tongue moved to tease the soft skin inside.

Logic, with a boost from self-preservation, finally raised a voice loud enough to startle Jade back to sanity. The frail strength of her palms, combined with the element of surprise, produced enough power to push Cain away.

"Jade?" This time the tone of his question leaned toward puzzlement or perhaps disbelief. When he took a step forward to recapture her in his embrace, she maneuvered deftly out of his reach.

"No, Mr. Delancy, no," she said, holding up her hand to ward off his advance. "If you assumed this kind of thing would work with me, you've got the wrong girl. I don't know the first thing about sex games."

His head angled to one side and his features crimped with bewildered annoyance. "Is that what we were doing just now, playing some kind of sex game?"

"I have no doubt that's what you were doing," she returned accusingly. "I see now that you never meant to let me have the painting—on any terms. You merely intended to play with me awhile."

"Play with you?" Anger eclipsed his features, bringing the sudden blackness of a cloud blown across the moon.

"Yes, play," she reiterated, "probably to find out how far I'd go to get that painting from you. I guess my bluff about buying it caught you by surprise, and you let down your guard for a moment. Obviously, this was your way of gaining back control. And I have to admit, you're very good at it," she proclaimed in a voice edged with scorn.

"The trouble is, you chose the wrong weapon this time. I told you before, I don't like being used."

"You don't think much of me, do you, Jade? Or is it that you don't trust men in general?" She felt the sting of his sarcastic backlash.

"I don't know enough about men to make that kind of judgment," she said, choosing to ignore the personal part of his question.

"Don't tell me I've just made a pass at a virgin?" Astonishment rooted out both sarcasm and anger in this solicitation. "You looked fairly young this afternoon, I'll admit. But when that hotel room door opened this evening, a woman full grown stood there." His gaze licked over the curves of her body with gourmet satisfaction.

"I'm twenty-five—today, as a matter-of-fact." Even as she voiced the defiant retort, she knew he'd seen in her eyes the truth about her innocence. "But this has pretty much taken care of any hope for many happy returns." She swiped trembling fingers across her tear-splotched cheeks and raised her chin in one final attempt to salvage her dignity. "If you don't mind, I'd like to go back to my hotel now."

Her abrupt termination of their conversation confounding him for a second, when he spoke, he fumbled for words. "Jade, I—can't we—?"

"No, Mr. Delancy," she cut in, "this is over. Now take me home—please."

He opened his mouth to say something else, but she raised impervious features against him like a warning flag. He let out his breath in an exasperated sigh and nodded toward the door.

During the drive back to her hotel, strained silence sat like an obstinate intruder between them. Jade permitted Cain to escort her upstairs to her room, but as soon as they reached her door, she squelched any softening of their parting with an abrupt, "Goodbye, Mr. Delancy."

When she closed the door behind her, she fully expected never to see Cain Delancy again.

"Damn it!" The anger inside directed at himself this time, Cain gritted his teeth and pounded his fists against the steering wheel. Convinced that she would eventually respond like any other woman to his powers of seduction; instead, during the past few hours, he'd allowed Jade Hartman to drag him through a gamut of emotions from frustration to lust to shame and, ultimately, to a feeling so intense he didn't dare put a name to it.

He felt his anger suck dry as a desperation more acute than he'd experienced this afternoon pounded at his gut. He had to do something—fast. Her appearance bordering on ethereal visitation, already Jade Hartman seemed about to disappear.

CHAPTER THREE

"No, not yet, please," Jade groaned, blinking awake. When, despite her protests, the ringing continued, she pushed aside a swath of golden hair and peeked at the bedside clock. Six a.m. Too early for the wakeup call she'd arranged for last evening. Oblivious to its mistake, however, the phone continued its incessant ringing.

"Hello," she snapped into the raised receiver, "this had better be good," stifled on the tip of her tongue.

"I'm terribly sorry to bother you, Miss Hartman," said the tremulous voice at the other end of the line. "This is George Hedley, the hotel manager, speaking. We met yesterday, if you remember. It seems we have a problem with a party of guests who've just arrived, and we desperately need your help." The words tumbled out of the man's mouth in a single breath, as though he feared she might hang up before he finished.

"Oh, Mr. Hedley," Jade mumbled, trying to shake the mass of cobwebs from her brain. "My help? I don't understand."

"I believe I noticed yesterday on your registration card that you're an interpreter?" the manager inquired, instead of answering the question she'd put to him.

"Yes, that's right."

"Well, it seems we have some kind of mix-up regarding the accommodations for these guests," he said, then added at once, "They're quite upset," as if that clarified the purpose of his call.

"Don't they speak English?" she asked, still struggling to make sense of the manager's faulty command of it at the moment.

"Oh dear, I do beg your pardon." Her caller seemed even more flustered. "I'm not handling any of this very well, I'm afraid. It's just that I'm not accustomed to having so many people…" His voice trailed off into an incoherent jumble of self-admonishments.

However, before Jade could prompt him further, he sucked in a deep breath and continued in a more audible voice, "The members of this party are African, and apparently they speak only their native tongue." An impatient sigh tunneled through the telephone wire. "Whatever that native tongue is. Do you happen to speak any African dialects, Miss Hartman?"

"Yes, of course," she said, "I speak several."

The manager heaved another labored sigh. "Oh, thank heaven. Can you-I mean, would you mind coming down and see if you can straighten all this out? I know it's a great imposition, but—"

"I'll be down in a few minutes," she assured the frazzled caller before he lapsed into another apologetic dissertation.

Jade hung up the phone amid a flurry of "thank yous" and glanced at the slacks she had laid out for the morning. A traditional African might not approve, she decided, and hastily took stock of the rest of her wardrobe. The demure blouse and skirt she'd packed on top remained unwrinkled. Dressing in haste, she spared a few minutes to make her hair presentable and dab on a little lip gloss. Then she set off downstairs to see how she might assist the beleaguered hotel manager.

"Please don't let this take long," she begged to the empty walls, as the elevator descended the several floors to the lobby. Her confrontation with Cain Delancy last evening had cast a pall over what might have been a therapeutic holiday, and, for the first time, she couldn't wait to leave Atlanta. She would let him keep the painting for now, she'd decided. But she would seek an attorney's advice as soon as she got back to Washington. Mr. Delancy wouldn't take away any more of her dignity if she could help it.

The sight that greeted her in the lobby was enough to fluster even a trained professional, Jade had to admit. Dozens of expensive suitcases in all sizes were stacked like dominoes in front of the registration desk.

A giant of a man with ebony skin was in the midst of a confrontation with the manager. As though heedless of the lack of comprehension by his listener, the black man continued to wave his arms and boom out directives in rapid Kiswahili. Garbed in a colorful caftan traditional with his people, he possessed the dramatic presence a producer dreams of in his Othello. Several strikingly beautiful black women, dressed in smart Western costumes, contributed their shrill voices to the drama. His own immaculate uniform seeming to wilt before this onslaught, Mr. Hedley cowered behind the counter trying to sneak a look over the shoulder of the taller man while feigning attention. When he caught sight of Jade, he sighed the relief of Atlas when the weight of the world was lifted from his shoulders.

"*Hu jambo*," Jade interjected, beginning the customary Swahili greeting as she approached the group.

The shouting silenced and a dozen dark eyes turned in her direction. Stopping in front of the obvious leader of the entourage, she offered her hand deferentially and introduced herself in the properly respectful tone he might expect of a woman. When the big African reacted to her appearance with a pleased sigh, she asked if he would indulge her ignorance and explain his problem. He remained mute for seconds while his penetrating eyes scanned her from head to toe. Apparently finding her demeanor acceptable in all ways, he proceeded to explain the cause of his dilemma.

Patience a constant demand in her job, she listened while he spouted an endless list of the troubles that had besieged his party of travelers during recent hours. Eventually, she gleaned from his monologue a sense of what he wanted done. If she'd been faced by circumstances such as these a year ago, she might have been amused by this another example of how a man's chauvinism set him at odds with the opposite sex. However, recent experience had sobered her on that subject.

Holding fast to her controlled expression, she assured the African that she would relay his needs.

"It seems Mr. Muhaffa has recently taken a new wife," she explained, at once transferring her thinking to English when she turned to explain to the hotel manager. “The other four ladies are his wives, also. It seems they disapprove of his latest bride, and none of them is willing to share a suite with her.

“Therefore,” she continued to her still puzzled listener, “Mr. Muhaffa requests a change in the accommodations he reserved originally. He wants you to separate all the women, giving each a suite of her own. He claims his mental well-being depends on getting a little peace from this constant bickering.”

A huge breath briefly inflated Mr. Hedley’s thin cheeks, then popped out like an opened release valve on a pressure cooker.

“Oh, my goodness, is that what all this disturbance has been about?” he asked, the mettle restored to his wilted demeanor. “I thought we had done something to offend him. When the whole party arrived without the interpreter I understood would keep close company with them at all times, I simply didn’t know how to handle it.

“Please tell Mr. Muhaffa, if you would be so kind, Miss Hartman,” he said with renewed supplication in his tone, “that we’ll be happy to grant his wishes. I’ll get the desk staff on it right away. We should have something worked out that will suit in just a few minutes. In the meantime, perhaps you might persuade the gentleman and his party to be our guests at breakfast. When we have the suites prepared, we can contact him in the restaurant.”

The black man’s understanding immediate when Jade relayed Mr. Hedley’s suggestions, his features softened into a smile that showed a set of pearly white teeth. He nodded his acceptance of the manager’s breakfast invitation, then turned to offer a few calming remarks to his ladies.

“Ah-uh, Miss Hartman,” Mr. Hedley ventured hesitantly when she confirmed that his guests had been placated for the time being, “I wonder, would you mind…?”

“Of course, I’ll accompany them to breakfast,” she said, anticipating his next request, “but you do understand I’m leaving today.”

“Oh, I’ve already alerted the people Mr. Muhaffa was supposed to meet here,” he assured her, “and I’m certain they’ll make arrangements for a new interpreter. Thank you so much for your help this morning. I don't know how I would have managed without you. You've saved my life." By this time Jade was becoming a little uncomfortable with the manager's praise which had graduated almost to homage.

"Ah, here's just the man who can carry on," he said, glancing over her shoulder.

His pale complexion lit up with pleased recognition. Before she could question him, he favored her with his attention again and elaborated, "Mr. Delancy was quite right to suggest that you were the person to handle the situation until he got here, Miss Hartman."

"Mr. Delancy?" Her mind resisting the idea that she'd heard right, Jade jerked her head around. Sure enough, making hasty strides in their direction was the man she'd never expected to see again. Perfectly groomed, still he looked more casual today dressed in grey slacks, blue blazer and open-collared shirt. He'd had time to create this immaculate appearance while she'd been left to "handle the situation," she thought with no small amount of irritation. While her mind denounced him, at the same time, her body felt again the lure of those cavalier goods looks, and she sensed his seductiveness hacking away at her defenses until the memory of his cruelty toward her last evening shoved reinforcements onto the barrier.

"Good morning, Jade," Cain said brightly. At once, he reacquainted her with that self-satisfied smile which had cued her on earlier occasions that he intended to get his way. "I take it you've already straightened out our little misunderstanding here?"

"Oh my yes, she has handled it splendidly," Mr. Hedley interjected before she had a chance to reply. "We were so fortunate that Miss Hartman was still with us."

"Yes, we were," Cain said, his eyes never leaving hers. "Now, perhaps the lady wouldn't mind introducing me to our African guests."

Jade fought back her initial urge to tell him to find another lackey to attend him (why he expected any favors from her she couldn't imagine) and performed the introductions. As soon as he recognized the newcomer's attachment to the Larkins, Mr. Muhaffa broke into another white-toothed grin and offered his hand to Cain. He commenced apologizing at once for disturbing his host at such an early hour. (Neither man seemed to consider it necessary to apologize to her.)

The exchange (with her technical assistance) between the two males soon revealed the purpose of the African's visit to Atlanta. He had agreed to negotiate with the Larkins for the possible sale of a number of pieces of cultural art that had come into his possession. *Crossroads of the World,* the Larkin's import company, would actually arrange for the purchase of the art. However, since Cain had already lined up buyers for several of the items, he had a considerable interest in the success of this venture.

Mr. Muhaffa apologized again for the problems of the morning. The interpreter who usually accompanied him had come down with a fever, he explained, and the authorities had placed the man in quarantine. Of course, Cain assured the African that he would make other arrangements for an interpreter before the day was out. As soon as Cain was informed of the delay in providing the extra suites requested, he renewed the invitation for everyone to pass the time at breakfast, with him coming along, as well, of course. The entire body seemed to expect that Jade would continue the role imposed on her earlier. Since her commitment to Mr. Hedley made it impossible to feed to her growing irritation and bow out of the proceedings, she conceded to complete the assignment she'd agreed to perform.

During breakfast, the two men carried on a raucous conversation with her as go-between. The African women didn't seem to mind being ignored by the men and carried on their own cheerful chatter. Though she understood every word uttered, nevertheless, Jade felt alienated by both groups.

This time it was pride that fired her resentment. Visiting dignitaries at the State Department had seldom included her in their active discussions. That had never bothered her. The translation of accurate information was her job and all parties made it known that they appreciated and respected her abilities. However, this was different;

she didn't work for Cain Delancy. Despite his behavior of last evening, he'd managed to trick her again by manipulating her into doing this as a favor. And now apparently he presumed he could use her as long as it suited him.

The group had barely finished their meal when Mr. Hedley darted into the room with the announcement that his guests' new quarters were ready. Pausing only long enough to make this one last translation, Jade seized the opportunity to slip away upstairs. She had a plane to catch, and the happenings of this morning had only strengthened her resolve to be on it. She had stowed the last of her things and just picked up the phone to ring downstairs for a bellboy when a knock sounded at the door.

"What is it this time, Mr. Delancy?" she asked coolly when she saw the man she couldn't seem to escape standing in her doorway. "I was about to leave for the airport."

Both dark eyebrows raised slightly. "Why do I have the feeling I've somehow offended you again, Jade?"

She shrugged. "It really doesn't matter."

"Of course it matters. I want to know. What's wrong?"

She lifted a defiant chin. "My feelings don't mean anything to you. You showed me that yesterday. Now, if you'll excuse me—"

She reached to close the door, but Cain's stronger hand was too quick. He'd pushed inside before she could block his way.

"I will *not* excuse you," he said almost like a threat.

"What do you want, Mr. Delancy?" she repeated in a voice salted with petulance.

"I came up here to thank you again for your help, Jade," he said in a tone that hardly sounded grateful. "And to—"

"So, now you've thanked me," she said, "you're welcome," but her continued grip on the doorknob belied the sincerity of the tacked-on cordiality.

His eyes still trained on hers, Cain pushed out one long arm and slammed the door shut. "What is it, Jade?" he asked in a quieter tone. "Tell me. How have I offended you this time?"

"You still don't understand, do you, Mr. Delancy? Even after what happened between us yesterday, it hasn't gotten through to you? Well, here it is as plain as I know how to make it—you used me, yesterday and again this morning." She fired the indictment at him in a voice as tight as a rubber band stretched to its limit. "I can overlook Mr. Muhaffa's chauvinist behavior. From what I know about his part of the world, men are conditioned to view women as objects they can summon at their convenience, then ignore in the presence of another male.

"But neither custom nor bond between us can excuse what you did. You have no claim to my professional services nor any other excuse to assume on my time. I solicited what I thought was a reasonable concession from you yesterday. For a time, you let me believe I might reason with you while you amused yourself at my expense. Then you turned down my request.

"Yet this morning," she continued before he could reply, "you didn't hesitate to solicit a favor from me. You knew I wouldn't refuse Mr. Hedley's plea, so you conspired with him to obtain my services for free. Then, as if that wasn't enough, you treated me like hired help in front of your guests. Using me that way was insensitive, not to mention rude. You've proved to me that you're totally incapable of empathy with the feelings of another human being. Just as you did when you displayed a painting which holds me up to public ridicule."

Jade turned away, suddenly aware that she'd given him yet another tool he could use to perforate the paper-thin veneer covering her emotions.

"Never mind," she mumbled. "Like I said, you wouldn't understand."

"I'll try." He'd moved so close that when he leaned toward her, she felt the stroke of his warm breath gentle on her neck. "Please, Jade." He reached out and clasped her shoulders gently. "Tell me. I want to know."

"No! you don't want to know." She jerked around so quickly the momentum ripped her from his grasp. She stared at him through a thick glaze of pain. "You don't really want to know. You've hung some unknown artist's creation in your gallery. The face he painted happens to match mine. You seem to want me to weave some romantic tale around its origin, perhaps to attract a higher price. But the only things I can tell you are ugly."

"I only want to know the truth," he said.

At first, Jade followed her mind's reflex and backed away. However, when she felt the edge of a chair touch the back of her knees, she realized at once the futility of physical retreat.

The painting had blocked her mental retreat, as well, she understood in the same second. By some strange coincidence, Cain Delancy had displayed it just at this time, transforming it into an emblem of her guilt as blatant as Hester Prynne's scarlet letter. She might as well confess her shame. Cain wouldn't sympathize but, at least, he might finally comprehend why she had to have the painting.

The tax on her energy suddenly too great to support her own weight, she sank into the chair behind her. When she spoke, she directed her words as much to herself as to her listener.

"My mother kept me ignorant of the ways of the world for a lot of my life," Jade said in opening. "She had suffered through some great ordeal when she was younger. She would never share it with me, but I knew she'd never gotten over it. I guess she wanted to spare me the cruelties of life for as long as she could. She'd meant to save me, but all it accomplished was to cripple me.

"You had to be told this first to show you that I had very little opportunity to learn life's rules ahead of time. So, when I did have to deal with my emotions for the first time, I got myself entangled in an affair, an ill-chosen one, one I couldn't handle. And, as a result, I hurt someone very badly."

"A lover?" Cain spoke up. He'd been listening intently and the question seemed more than idle curiosity. "You were involved with a man and you hurt him, is that it?"

She interrupted her memory with a fleeting glance at her questioner. "I was involved with a man, but he isn't the one I'm talking about." She heaved a heavy sigh.

"Bonn Corbett," she mused aloud, "funny how that name sounded so impressive at the time. He was the man," she added to clarify.

"Last year the State Department transferred Bonn to our division when a management position became vacant." She glanced again at Cain, curious to see if he showed any sign of recognizing the name. When she saw no change in his expression, "Bonn was one of those worldly men I'd only read about in books," she said. "I still can't believe how ignorant I was," she added in self-admonishment.

"I was infatuated with him from the first," she said when her listener nodded for her to continue. "Of course, I never really expected anything would come of it. After all, why should a man like him notice me? Eventually, though, he must have become aware of my fawning attentions because he began to invent excuses to talk to me. Then one day he asked me out. I was so thrilled I never stopped to question his motives.

"He seemed interested in hearing about me. I was flattered. Most men I'd known only seemed interested in talking about themselves. But each time we talked, our conversation seemed to end up on something related to work, important conferences the State Department had scheduled, that sort of thing. I didn't notice anything particularly wrong about that, though. Bonn was my superior. I assumed he'd been briefed on most things that went on in the division, anyway. Then one day he asked me about a specific assignment of mine, a special meeting that had been kept very hush-hush. I laughed and told him he should know I couldn't discuss anything about that one. He laughed, too, and dropped the subject.

"But he didn't drop it," Cain guessed, seeing at once what she hadn't noticed.

"Far from it. But his cover was almost perfect. He asked me something else the very next day—not about work, though. He asked if I would go away with him for the weekend. I guess he knew I wouldn't refuse that request. He had to have seen in my face my feelings for him. And, of course, I didn't refuse.

"He took me to this beautiful place in the Catskills. We'd just checked into the hotel, and I'd gone to the bedroom of our suite to change from my traveling clothes when I remembered I'd left my overnight case in the sitting room. I opened the door just in time to overhear Bonn talking to someone on the phone. He said not to worry, he'd get the details about the special conference from me before the weekend was out." Jade met Cain's intense gaze for the first time. "I'd nearly given myself, body and soul, to a man who cared nothing about me, who intended merely to use me for his own purposes. Once he got me in bed, he must have thought it would be easy to coax me into revealing the political secrets he wanted. I learned later that he planned to sell the information to a foreign power."

"Did you report him?" Cain asked.

"I slammed into the room threatening to do that very thing. He just laughed. He said it would be very upsetting to his wife if I told anybody about this."

"His wife? He was married?" Cain's outspoken query indicated he'd been unprepared for this latest twist.

"I hadn't bothered to ask, can you believe it?" Her tremulous chuckle echoed in the silence. "My shocked reaction didn't impress Bonn. He accused me of knowing about his wife all along. Women always know those things, he said.

"Bonn's wife was the daughter of a career military man," she went on before Cain could comment. "He informed me of that as though it were some kind of shield from harm. The colonel had sponsored his son-in-law's career, you see. If I told anyone what Bonn had planned to do, I'd have to reveal that I'd gone off for a weekend with another woman's husband. The scandal of that alone would disgrace his wife and possibly damage his father-in-law's career—not to mention my reputation would be in shambles."

"Good God, what a spot to find yourself," Cain blurted in a tone that included as much sympathy as astonishment. "What did you do?"

"I grabbed my suitcases and left. I got home on my own, of course, then spent the rest of the weekend wrestling with my conscience. Finally, I made the only decision I thought I'd be able to live with—I went to Bonn's wife and told her the whole story. After I'd finished, I explained I had no choice but to inform the authorities, as well."

Cain nodded, as though he'd guessed the course she had chosen. "How did his wife take the news?" he prompted.

"She didn't seem surprised about our affair. She said it wasn't the first fling her husband had engaged in. Men tended to stray from time to time, she accepted that. But what she didn't understand was why I thought I had to report what I'd overheard at the hotel. She practically begged me to let it go."

"But you couldn't let it go?" Cain seemed to know that, too.

Jade shook her head. "I couldn't have lived with it. Even if he hadn't succeeded with me, who's to say Bonn wouldn't have found another way to obtain information he could sell. I'd sworn an oath when I accepted my job and I had to protect that integrity.

Of course, the government agents I spoke to didn't believe me at first. But I'd overheard the name of the man Bonn had been talking to on the phone—it was Korean. They'd seen the same name on one of their spy lists so they had to investigate. Sure enough, they uncovered witnesses to Bonn's attempts in the past to sell information." Through eyes dewy with unshed tears, she forced herself to look directly at Cain. "I'm surprised you never read about any of this. The scandal was splashed over all the papers."

"I was out of the country a lot this spring," he said. "I guess the story broke while I was away."

Tears had begun to spill onto Jade cheeks by now. Cain moved closer and knelt beside her chair. Hesitating, as if uncertain whether he should touch her, finally he reached up and pressed his handkerchief into her hand, then withdrew.

"You mustn't feel so guilty, Jade," he said, the words falling clumsily from his lips. "You only did what you had to do."

Uncomforted by his attempt at solace, she swallowed hard and began to speak again. "Even that wasn't the end of the whole sorted mess. The exposure of his son-in-law brought the colonel's whole career under scrutiny. Had he covered for his daughter's husband before? the newspapers asked. Nothing was ever proven, at least no criminal acts on his part. But he'd sponsored Bonn's career in the State Department and that was enough to call his patriotism into question."

"So his military career was ruined?"

"His career, his personal life, everything, the way he saw it. The day Bonn was going to be arraigned in court, he took a gun and went to the federal courthouse and waited outside. When the federal marshals brought Bonn from the jail, he pushed close enough to fire one shot. He was an expert marksman; Bonn fell dead instantly. Then, in front of a stunned crowd of people, he turned the gun on himself and fired again."

Looking stunned himself by what he was hearing, Cain merely shook his head.

"I never dreamed so much harm could result from my foolishness," she continued. "Bonn's wife burst into my office the next morning screaming about how I'd 'killed' her whole family." Jade squeezed her eyelids tight, wringing more tears from her thick lashes. "I don't know, maybe I was responsible."

Cain's reaction to this was immediate. "No, Jade," he said, "you know better than that. Put the blame where it belongs, not with you."

She shrugged. "Anyway, I couldn't stand to work at the Department any longer. I didn't want to know any more secrets that might hurt people that way." She stared briefly at the handkerchief in her hand, not quite certain how it had gotten there. She turned and looked at Cain in earnest, searching for the truth of his evaluation of her story. He might absolve her from blame, but did he understand the depth of her pain? Or did he merely feel sorry for her as one would a wounded animal? "Bonn's wife said she wished she could hang a picture of me somewhere so all the world could see the rawness of my sin. Then I'd have to suffer the kind of humiliation she was having to endure. I guess she got her wish."

Cain pushed himself up from his knees and stood for moment looking into Jade's tear-streaked face. "I'm sorrier than I can tell you for what I did yesterday," he said at last. She watched as he fumbled through his pockets, finally extracting a scrap of paper. "What I really came up here for was to ask you to extend us your professional services for a few days while Mr. Muhaffa's in town.

"You said last night that you hadn't committed to that job in New York yet," he added when she didn't respond. "Why not let us hire you at whatever salary you think is reasonable while you decide your future?"

When Jade continued to stare at him in silence, "Cy and Leona have been counting on these purchases," he explained further. "And I have customers who're expecting me to produce the pieces. This glitch could cause the whole deal to fall through. Muhaffa doesn't strike me as a patient man. He may pack up that entourage of his and leave town before we can arrange for another interpreter. Won't you consider taking the job for Cy and Leona's sake, if not for mine?"

Skepticism took the place of pain in Jade's features. "And what kind of strings are attached to this request?" she asked.

She saw his brow pinch slightly. "No strings, Jade," he said. "I'm just making you a straightforward offer of employment. And, by the way, I'd already considered the position retroactive to this morning. I never meant to treat you disrespectfully, I promise you.

"Think about it, will you? You can reach me at the gallery." He unfolded the scrap of paper he'd extracted from his pocket earlier. "Whatever you decide, this is for you." He handed her the paper. "It gives you title to the painting." That enigmatic half-smile made an appearance. "Consider it a late birthday gift."

"I can't let you do that." She tried to hand the paper back to him, but he folded her fingers around it and shook his head.

"Take it," he said. "By rights, the painting should be yours. I realized that after we talked last night. Just let me know where you want it sent." Suddenly, as if his gesture made him uncomfortable, he turned and walked toward the door.

"Cain." Jade's speaking of his name was as spontaneous as her decision. He stopped and glanced back at her over his shoulder. "When do I report for work?"

CHAPTER FOUR

"I need you right now."

For a man practiced in mocking expressions, Cain exhibited remarkable talent with a real smile. "Would you mind?" he asked, turning to reward Jade with a prime example. "I'd like to get these meetings with Muhaffa started today, if we can," he mulled aloud. "Arranging it without his wives around may be a problem, of course."

"How about setting up a private showing for the ladies in the hotel with some of the more exclusive dress shops," she suggested, at once finding solace from her pain inside a cloak of professionalism. "They look like women who enjoy clothes and they should find shopping more appealing than a boring business meeting. At breakfast I discovered that Mr. Muhaffa's most recent bride speaks a little English, so the women should be able to manage for one day without an interpreter."

"Good girl." The relief in Cain's expression blossomed into admiration. "I should have known an expert like you could come up with a plan. We can order lunch for the ladies ahead of time and have the restaurant set up a buffet. As for the showings, I'm sure Leona will know how to take care of that part."

Her hands clasped inside his, the next second Jade found herself on her feet staring into his dark eyes. He stood for a moment gazing into the liquid jade. Then he shook his head and released her.

"Well, now that we've got that settled," he said, resuming his enthusiastic tone, "dry your eyes and let's see if we can get this show on the road."

"Sorry," she said, at once self-conscious. She dabbed at her wet cheeks with his handkerchief and handed it back. "I must look a fright."

Cain reached out and touched a strand of her hair. As if he might permit himself this one indulgence, he sifted the silken locks through his fingers. "You couldn't look any way except beautiful," he murmured.

Since she had no words in any language to test his sincerity when he spoke like that, she opted to remain on the one level of this relationship where truth had touched.

"Thanks for giving me the painting, Cain," she said, risking a hesitant smile to supplement her words of gratitude. Before he could answer, she turned away and escaped into the bathroom.

While he walked alongside Jade down the hotel corridor, at the same time, Cain sent up silent words of thanks to the powers that be. Hoping the gift of the painting might serve as a peace offering, he'd meant to come to her this morning with an appeal to stay a few days longer so they could talk again. Now a fortunate accident had furnished another purpose for her to remain. She would stay—for a few more days, at least.

Risking a glance at his companion, his eyes begged the question he must find the answer to: Who was she? She looked so fragile, yet he recognized now a remarkable strength in her. The injustices she'd suffered during recent months were greater than anyone should have to bear. Her pain touched him in a way he hadn't known he could feel. No wonder she took the image in the painting so personally.

His empathy aside, what she'd revealed about herself, in both words and actions, provided him with hope for his own cause. Though she became offended easily when she thought she'd been used, hers was an inherently responsive nature.

She didn't respond to aggressive physical advances, though. Now he knew why; she didn't even understand the power of her own sensuality. On the contrary, she was as suspect of her appeal as a woman as she was of his intentions. His best chance for building trust was to let her discover on her own the sensual attraction that was her natural gift. In return, perhaps she would give him the information he sought as a personal favor to a friend—a very close friend.

The rest of the morning went well. Her profession the one area where Jade felt sure of herself, she executed her duties with consummate skill. At first, Mr. Muhaffa's wives didn't like the idea of being left behind. However, after Jade explained the treat in store for them, they started up a fresh clatter of excited anticipation. Mr. Muhaffa won quite a few accolades himself when he granted his spouses permission to purchase whatever they wanted.

Jade had guessed that the newest wife's youth was the main reason the other ladies resented her. At the first opportunity, she drew the girl discreetly aside. Relying on the shared intuition of women, she suggested in English that the new Mrs. Muhaffa encourage the clothiers this once to show the older women their more attractive outfits. The young bride understood immediately and smiled her thanks.

"You may find Mr. Muhaffa easier to deal with if his women aren't giving him so much trouble," Jade whispered to Cain while their guests gathered to discuss items in their wardrobes that they considered outdated

"I certainly would be more amiable," he whispered back. The look she glimpsed from the corner of her eye indicated his reply had little to do with the problems of the big African.

Cy and Leona appeared just ahead of the clothiers. Within minutes, Jade saw that there was further need for her to oversee the proceedings. As soon as Leona understood the situation, she'd agreed to remain to make sure the exhibition continued smoothly, and Cy was taking care of the luncheon arrangements with the hotel chef.

Cain's parents seemed surprised that Jade had consented to stay and furnish them with her interpreting skills. Nevertheless, before she exited with Cain, Leona made a point of thanking her for delaying her departure on their behalf.

"I've already asked Jade to dinner again at the house," Cain interjected, turning to appeal to his mother. "Don't let her turn us down, will you. I know you'd intended to ask Mr. Muhaffa and his party to be our guests. But I'm betting he'll prefer a more intimate dinner since his wives should be in a very good mood for a change. Please convince Jade that we want her with us," he added clumsily. Supplication seemed a stranger to those lips from which demands for acquiescence seemed to come easily.

"I don't think I should impose," Jade managed to insert before Leona came back with, "My dear, you must join us. We're anxious to know you better and we hardly got the chance to become acquainted last evening."

Jade might have argued that she'd learned more about this family last evening than she cared to, but Cain's recent behavior had been to his credit. His gift alone hadn't erased her wariness of him; it was his acceptance of her pitiful story without recriminations (something she couldn't say for many of the people she'd considered friends back in Washington) which had softened her toward him more than anything. So, because his parents had made her welcome and because it would be less than gracious to refuse such an avid appeal, she agreed to another dinner at the Larkins.

After their business with Muhaffa was finished for the day, Cy extended the anticipated invitation for the whole entourage to dine with his family and got the polite refusal Cain had predicted. Then, as if he feared she might yet disappear, Cain insisted on escorting Jade to her suite, then waited while she changed for dinner. During the drive to his house, she concentrated on shoring up her defenses. While the sympathetic behavior her companion had displayed earlier attracted her senses like a romantic to a fictional hero, she knew the danger his physical potency imposed was still very real.

The return of their guest of the evening before seemed to please everyone in the Larkin household. Nevertheless, throughout the meal, Cain continued last night's ritual of watching silently while Cy and Leona carried the conversation. Jade could only surmise that, for some reason, he was reluctant to reveal anything personal about himself in front of his foster parents. Could some actual feeling of vulnerability be the cause?

His mention yesterday of a brother came to mind; perhaps his parents had somehow slighted Cain in favor of the other sibling. When the elders left the two of them alone later in the evening, her curiosity nudged enough to ask about it.

"Your parents seem like nice people," she commented, when they were ensconced on a rear veranda outside of the hearing of the household. Not wanting to sit just yet, she'd paused to study the patterns of stars decorating the night sky.

"Yes, I guess they're okay," she heard in a vague undertone. He'd taken her cue and now stood just behind her on the porch.

Turning to face him, "The different last names," she ventured, "I've been wondering, are you an adopted son?"

"In a manner of speaking," he answered in a repeat of that phrase she'd heard during their first meeting.

"Your brother, is he also adopted?" she continued.

"No, he's the Larkins' natural son. He was born four years before I came to live with them."

"Oh, I see." But her polite response directly contradicted her thoughts. "So, Delancy was your biological father's name?"

He shrugged. "I haven't the faintest idea."

Assuming she'd already encroached too far along a path Cain seemed to prefer she not travel, Jade backed off the subject.

"Your gallery must be doing well," she observed, partly out of curiosity and partly in search of a safer topic of conversation. "I mean, if you can afford to pass up a hundred thousand dollar offer on a painting…"

Another shrug. "Don't worry about it. I don't mind the financial loss, and Cy and Leona don't care whether I make money on the gallery or not."

After that, Jade quieted completely. With every effort to avoid a misstep on the subject of Cain's relationship with his family, she seemed to put her foot on another faulty plank. Uncertain about what her host expected of her, she fiddled nervously with the pleats of her skirt. However, when she moved toward one of the chairs, Cain touched her arm.

"Don't sit down, please," he said. The courtesy hadn't been dragged reluctantly from his lips this time, she noticed. "Let's walk in the garden for awhile."

A walk alone with him in the moonlight. Suddenly, Jade was alerted to her own vulnerable state. So far this evening, Cain hadn't committed any trespass to trigger her wariness. On the contrary, his behavior of late had reduced the effects of yesterday considerably. This morning, he'd managed to breach her defenses and had edged through them so skillfully she had lost some of her fear of him. Only months ago, another dangerous man had captured her senses and nearly ripped her heart to pieces. Dare she risk putting it again in harm's way?

"Please," Cain repeated to her undoing.

"All right, but let me get my jacket," she said, congratulating herself for having thought of this small excuse to regain control of her senses. "I've felt a slight chill during the past few minutes," she added in a kind of truth. "No, I know just where I left it," she said, raising her hand in protest when he turned to go in her stead.

Watching Jade glide away into the star-spangled night, Cain tried once more to make peace with his feelings. All her movements were like that; she seemed to materialize in front of him and vanish just as easily. Her slightest touch a pin's prick to his desire, he'd had to summon every reserve of control to hold back any overt demonstration of the wildness clamoring inside him.

But each time he saw her, he nearly lost his battle. Since she'd first appeared in his office yesterday, an ever increasing demand to touch her had enveloped his body. Never had a flesh and blood woman provoked such a powerful stimulus to his senses.

In the past, his pursuit of women had resulted in a number of flash fires that burned white-hot for a brief space of time, then disappeared into the blaze of their own energies. Maybe he lacked the lasting feelings other men eventually discovered within themselves. Or perhaps he'd merely developed a more realistic philosophy concerning passionate emotions—that no mortal can capture and hold them for long—except perhaps on a piece of canvas.

He felt an increasing urgency to hold onto this woman, though. The answers she might give him still mattered, yet her effect on him reached beyond that. He had to find a way to get closer to her without triggering her wariness.

Maybe if he shared with her a few more bits of the truth…

"Ready?" Cain asked, seeming to come to himself when Jade touched his arm.

She nodded and, with almost reverent gentleness, he wrapped her slender fingers around his arm and urged her close enough to share the warmth of their bodies.

"You showed me a lot about who you are this morning," he said, as they started down the garden path. "I guess I owe it to you to return the favor."

"You don't owe me any explanations," she said, but inwardly she felt surprise that he'd volunteered any part of himself to her. "I hadn't meant to pry earlier. It's just that Cy and Leona seem like such nice people."

"They *are* nice people. Apparently, I'm not, though."

"What?" She halted in mid-step and turned to stare into his face. The matter-of-factness of his tone astounded her as much as the bluntness of his statement. The moon's ghostly light diluted his dark features. Or was the change more than just the light? "Why would you say such a thing?"

"You asked me if I was adopted," he offered in explanation. "I cut you off before but I want to try to answer you now. You see, Cy and Leona took me in when I was about two years old. I remember practically nothing about my life before that time, and they've refused to give me any direct answers when I question them about it.

"I can't really fault them for their care of me otherwise. I even thought I shared in everything they'd provided for their natural son—until I discovered it wasn't true." In the pale moonlight, the pain etched into his brow might have escaped her notice, had not the catch in his voice alerted her. "They'd never given me their name."

That explained a lot, Jade thought, a wave of sympathy washing away more of her suspicions. The Larkins had taken Cain into their home and given him all the material privileges of a son, but, for whatever reason, they'd never gifted him with their name.

"Have they ever said why they didn't make you their son?" she put to him aloud.

He shook his head. "Not really. All they'll say is they're not free to change anything or answer my questions about it. They say when I receive my share of their estate I'll be told the whole story."

"Aren't they at all sensitive to the way that makes you feel?"

"I guess it makes some difference to them. They keep insisting their omission doesn't mean their feelings for me aren't those of a true son. And, I have to admit, I can't point to anything concrete that should make me suspect their motives."

"Then, wouldn't it be better if you did as they asked and left it alone?" Jade offered reasonably.

"Maybe," he said. "But I can't seem to shake the feeling that they're hiding something, something ugly, and that's the real reason they've acted the way they have."

"So, what are you going to do?"

"About them? I don't know. I've told them I prefer that they just forget about any legacy I might have coming and sell me the gallery. I know that sounds harsh," he said when she grimaced, "but it's the only thing I really think of as mine.

"I was a kid fresh out of college when I took over running the place. Cy and Leona had owned it ever since I could remember, but they'd never seemed to take much notice of how it was run. The guy they'd hired as a manager was so incompetent he barely sold enough pieces to pay the bills. I've built that gallery into a successful enterprise and made them a good deal of money in the process. I've even drawn up plans for expansion that could incorporate more of the pieces they acquire through their import business."

"How did they react to your offer to buy the gallery?" Jade asked.

"With another put-off. Oh, they don't dispute that it should belong to me. They claim it's part of the legacy that will be mine someday. But they won't allow me to own it on any terms before that time."

He looked away, but not before Jade saw the pain re-enter that perfectly sculpted face. She'd been wrong this morning; Cain Delancy did understand how it felt to have people use him. Their generosity toward him notwithstanding, Cy and Leona Larkin had caused him to view their relationship in just that way. Surely, his foster parents had sound reasons for what seemed the unkindest cut of all—to refuse him their name.

Maybe there was a legitimate reason for it. Sometimes adoptive parents agreed to unusual stipulations. But Cain wouldn't feel any less an outsider if she reminded him of that now.

What could she do to pull him from this void of aloneness? He might misconstrue physical contact. He was a volatile man, as well as a potently sexual one, harboring an unrequited anger that could backlash if she acted recklessly. No, physical intimacy posed too great a risk. Yet her heart nudged her to reach out to him in some way.

"I'd like to hear about your plans for expanding the gallery before I leave," she said. "You must find it fascinating to work with wonderful pieces of art every day."

"Would you really like to hear about that?" The thin blanket of sarcasm didn't conceal his surprise at her interest. "I thought you didn't approve of what I do."

"Why would I disapprove of sharing art with the world?" she said, surprise volleying back into her court. "That's not true, at all. I didn't just wander into your gallery yesterday to escape the sultry weather outside. On the whole, I'm a true lover of art. In fact, visiting art galleries is one of my favorite pastimes. My mother taught me to recognize and appreciate great works of art from the time I was a small child. I've even managed to purchase a few inexpensive paintings. I've always wished I could afford to own a really important piece."

"Well, you own at least one now," he reminded her.

"Yes, I guess I do." She realized he referred to the circumstances of his gift of a painting he could have sold for a small fortune. Hastily, she lowered her eyelashes in an attempt to escape his penetrating gaze.

But she didn't manage it. Cain reached out and balanced her small chin on the crook of his index finger. Her eyelashes lifted reflexively.

"Hey, I didn't mean that as a criticism," he chided gently. "You should own that painting. You've paid for it just by coming to me. I've been hoping some twist of fate might make something like this happen."

"I don't know what you mean."

"Whoever posed for the painting had a face that inspired the artist to greatness. If I'd been able to find her, I would have given it to her. But since it couldn't happen, I'm glad I could give it to you."

For long moments, he stared at her in silence. However, when she thought he might satisfy the dark craving in his eyes and kiss her, he pulled away.

"Would you really like to know more about the gallery?" he asked with an obvious effort to clear his throat. His query sounded cordial and sincere this time.

"Yes, I would," she answered without hesitation.

"Well, if you'll walk with me a few more steps, I'd like to show you something."

Her gaze followed in the direction he pointed to a small white cottage. "This property has a couple of guest houses. I use the larger one as my living quarters when I stay over here."

Jade wanted to ask him why he chose to behave like a guest at his own parents' home, but suspected she already knew the answer.

Strangely undisturbed when his hand cupped her elbow, she allowed Cain to guide her toward the modest structure ahead. It possessed the quiet beauty of the simple saltbox design popular in colonial America. Moonlight coated the white wood siding with a platinum overlay, spilling more iridescent droplets on the tips of the bushes in front.

When they reached the small porch, Cain produced a key from his pocket and inserted it into the door lock. He shoved his hand through the opening and felt around for a light switch.

"Here we are," he said, as light flooded the room. "This is the place I call home."

The deluge of radiance revealed another incongruity among the many Jade had encountered with her host. The furnishings in this place he referred to as "home" were simple, almost Spartan. More than half the cottage consisted of one large room with a kitchen alcove tucked in the left rear corner. The two interior doors preceding that alcove closed off the only private rooms. Most of the space along the wall to the extreme right was taken up by a massive desk and a drafting board. Stacks of papers and blueprints cluttered both surfaces.

The hardwood floors, though highly polished, shunned any decoration. In fact, the only ornaments the room possessed were several unframed canvases.

Jade's wandering gaze snagged on a large crated object propped against the wall at the far end of the room.

"Your painting," Cain said in answer to her unasked question. "I'll see that it's shipped to you as soon as you provide me with an address."

An uncertain smile skittered across her lips. She hadn't quite believed until this moment that he meant to give up the painting. He'd kept his word to her.

Curiosity pushed her steps toward more canvases stacked against another wall. As she paused to study each one, she became aware of a very distinct similarity.

Whoever had produced these other unsigned works had, in a way similar to her own painting, captured his subjects in the throes of some heightened emotion. A craggy-faced man dressed in an ill-fitting suit watched his boy graduate, a young woman waved goodbye to a soldier outside a bus station, a ragged little girl peered at the dolls in a toy store window; they all emoted the same intense sensitivity. Perhaps it was in their eyes, maybe in the set of their mouths, she wasn't quite sure, but something in their faces was so intense it seemed to provide a glimpse into their souls.

"I'm not a painter myself, but I know a lot about art." Cain had moved to stand directly behind Jade. "I'm certain that whoever painted all these portraits was a great artist. He had the ability to capture intimate emotions better than any artist I've ever seen."

To illustrate his conclusion, her host placed his hands gently on her shoulders and directed her toward details in each painting she hadn't yet noticed. Then with the slightest pressure, he turned her around to face him.

"But you, Jade," he said, his gaze plunging into the boundless depths of her eyes, "you have one of those faces that mirrors a whole range of emotions at the same time. That's why I chose your painting for display. As good as these in front of you are, your portrait represents this artist's masterpiece."

"But it's not my portrait," she reminded him. "I just happen to look like someone in a painting. I'm nothing special."

"Yes, you are." His fingers tightened insistently on her shoulders. "You've tried to hide it, but I've seen it over and over ever since you marched into my office yesterday. Whenever you feel something deeply, that same rich play of emotions the artist captured in the painting appear in your face."

Sudden annoyance flared. "You mean you've actually tried to make me angry or sad just to test my responses?" she demanded.

"God, no." For a second, a look of panic spread over his countenance. "Of course not, that's not what I meant," he denied with more vehemence. "I've never intended to push you around like some puppet on a string. I've just observed you carefully over the last couple of days, that's all. And what I've seen has convinced me that your resemblance to the face in that picture is more than a coincidence. You must be able to tell me something about the woman. When I find her, then I'll know what I have to do to locate the artist."

Jade contemplated a moment whether truth lay behind those dark eyes. "I'm still certain I don't know anything that could help you," she said at last.

A glimmer of disappointment showed through in his features before he jerked down his mask of self-control.

"It's late, I'd better get you back to your hotel," he said to cover. When he stepped away from her, his shoulders sagged, as if he'd used up the last of his energy.

"However," she amended when he turned to usher her toward the door, "I don't see the harm in allowing you to ask me a few questions."

CHAPTER FIVE

"You're not sorry you agreed to this, are you?"

Jade detected concern in the tone of Cain's question as he leaned in to pull out her chair. No doubt, he'd seen the weariness in her features this evening. He'd become less reticent during these meals at his foster family's house, she'd noticed. Even so, most of his remarks were directed at her. Seating himself across from her now, he trained dark eyes on her face and repeated his question. "Are you sorry, Jade?"

"I just wish it was over with," she said, expelling a long sigh.

His tone became even more anxious. "But you will stay until we've finished with everything?"

"Give the girl a chance to catch her breath, son," Cy spoke up, himself more talkative of late. "We've been working her all day."

Jade looked gratitude at Cain's foster father. She did need a respite to realign her emotions.

She realized Cain's queries implied more than her language expertise with their African client. He wanted assurance that she hadn't changed her mind about the agreement she'd made with him privately. Their energies focused all week on talks that could evolve into a very lucrative deal for African art, Cain had had little opportunity to get her alone long enough to pose the questions he seemed to think she could answer.

His queries (which she still believed would bear no fruit) did not worry her. However, continued close contact with his potent masculinity did. Without the wariness of their early acquaintance to reinforce her defenses, she felt more vulnerable than ever each time he was near.

And her face, what a betrayer it was! As he'd told her often, her features were a catalog of her feelings. Had she already given away too much to save herself from falling in love with him? To his credit, he'd kept his hands off her except in the courtesies. But when these negotiations with Mr. Muhaffa came to a close, what would be left to hold him off then? His need to question her about who might be the possible subject of the painting? How long could she continue to plead ignorance in the matter before he gave up and turned his attention to other interests?

"I hope you aren't really thinking about leaving us," Leona said after the first course of the meal had been served. "We've so enjoyed having you here."

"I made a promise to stay until my contribution is completed, and I will," Jade assured everyone at the table. "I'm just a little impatient with all Mr. Muhaffa's haggling."

Leona glanced at Cy and they shared a laugh. "Oh, my dear girl," she said, "we're so used to haggling over prices with clients we hadn't even realized how aggravating it can be to someone who's not in the business. In Mr. Muhaffa's part of the world that's the way people conduct their financial transactions."

"Muhaffa would lose face if he gave in too soon," Cy offered. "We men must protect our egos, you know."

Jade let a smile smooth away some of her fatigue. Cain's father had a lot to say, she had observed, when business matters were involved. Both he and Leona had become completely at ease in her presence. Apparently, they now accepted that she'd agreed to remain in Atlanta while the African entourage was in town simply because they required her skills. They'd even insisted that she move into the second guest cottage for the duration of her stay. Free room and board appealed to her as much as comfort, she had to admit when she'd agreed to accept.

"It's the reason we started the bidding for the art at such a low figure," Cy continued in his explanation of the bargaining strategy they were compelled to employ with a man like Muhaffa. "We had to keep him interested."

"I see." Jade didn't know how prices for art pieces were agreed upon, but she remembered Mr. Muhaffa's graphic reaction to Cy's initial offer. "I guess you've had a lot of experience with this sort of thing."

"We've been in the import business for what," he glanced at his wife, "thirty-five years?"

She nodded. "It's taken us a long time to develop a network of contacts around the world. We actually lived in France for awhile years ago."

Jade perked with renewed interest. "How fascinating! As it happens, I was brought up in France. My mother still lives there."

What had started as a casual exchange suddenly brought an ominous quiet to the room. Leona's fair complexion blanched nearly white. The look she traded with her husband this time was heavily weighted with the old suspicion.

Cain, on the other hand, seemed amused by something. The smugness in his grin disturbed Jade.

"So, you say you grew up in France?" He directed the query at Jade, except, she noticed, the repeat of her childhood home was stabbed in his parents' direction. "I knew I detected a slight foreign accent. Tell me about your family." He barbed another glance at the Larkins. "I, for one, would like to hear everything about them."

Confused, nonetheless, Jade saw no reason not to comply. So she commenced a description of her childhood and the life her parents had provided in a small town outside Paris. She spoke with pride of the contribution her father had made to the medical field and of her mother's unwavering support of his work.

Dr. Jason Hartman had developed a promising career in the field of restorative surgery before her parents met, her mother had told her. However, after a congenital heart defect slowed his energies, he'd abandoned an active practice in the States and devoted his remaining years to research with skin grafts.

Since she'd been barely five years old when he died, Jade remembered him primarily through her mother's fond reminiscences. Her young years after her father's passing had been divided between the secluded existence at her mother's small villa in the French hamlet near Paris and various schools in the city. Although Kellus Hartman was herself an educated woman, she seemed to prefer her cloistered life and, even now, she seldom traveled far beyond their village.

Back at her own cottage later that evening, Jade puzzled over the effect her comments about herself had produced at the dinner table. Cain, especially. He'd seemed attentive to every word she uttered, as if sifting her revelations for useful facts. This whole matter between him and his parents still baffled her. Likewise, she suspected Cain had more reasons than he'd told her for his fixation with a portrait. And she felt certain he sought something else from her besides the identity of its painter.

Regardless of any secret agenda he might have, he'd followed through on his promise to turn over the painting to her. When she'd moved into the second guest house earlier this week, the crate awaited her. Unable to fully understand why, nevertheless, she'd felt compelled to open the crate and take another look at the face in the picture.

Was Cain right? she'd asked herself after she pried open the wooden cover and once again beheld her own image staring back at her. Did more than coincidence lie behind that face? Did the woman in the portrait share some kinship with her?

She'd decided not to destroy it, not yet, anyway. She'd removed a print from the wall beside her bed and hung the painting in its place. It didn't fit the setting, of course; a canvas like that needed a large room with a higher ceiling. But this location would do for the few days of her stay here. She'd studied it every day since, and each time she hoped she might spot something else about it that looked familiar.

When Jade finally dropped off to sleep that evening, she dreamed about a woman whose face matched her own who kept beckoning to her to follow. Yet, when she tried to comply, the woman moved away into the forest like some elusive wood nymph.

"Can't I have just one day away from this madness?"

Jade finished tying the ribbon through her hair and hurried to answer the knock at her door. After yesterday's grueling work schedule and the strained atmosphere at dinner last evening, she'd counted on having this small space of time for herself. Mr. Muhaffa and his entourage had gone to visit friends in New York for the weekend so no one should require her translating services. Had some new business emergency arisen?

When she opened the door, however, the man standing before her looked as if business was the last thing on his mind.

"Good morning." A picnic basket slung over one arm, Cain hardly resembled the grim character who had sat across the dinner table from her last evening. He looked totally relaxed in his hip-hugging jeans and pullover knit shirt. He gifted her with one of those rare, genuine smiles. "How about some lunch out in the fresh air?" he asked, waving the wicker basket enticingly in front of her.

"I think we owe ourselves a few hours off," he continued when she fixed him with a quizzical stare. "The housekeeper packed us some food." He embellished his sales pitch with an appreciative glimpse inside the basket. "Looks good. What do you say? Want to join me?"

She had to hand it to him; he'd lost no time figuring a way to get her off someplace alone. His appetite whetted last evening by the information she'd revealed, did he assume she would satisfy his hunger for more personal revelations? Or did he hope to satisfy other appetites which, likewise, had nothing to do with food?

"What did you have in mind?" she asked, hesitating. "For lunch, I mean," she amended when she realized she'd committed another slip-of-the tongue.

If he recognized an opportunity to mock her wariness, he let it pass. "I have some property about ten miles outside of town," he explained. "A fellow named Jim Scott has approached me about harvesting the pine timber on it. He wants to meet out there today to discuss it. Our meeting shouldn't take long, though. Afterward, I thought we might find a nice spot under some big trees and have our lunch. How about it, come with me?" His grin looked amazingly without guile.

The invitation sounded innocent, as well. What had she expected him to say, though? That he intended to spirit her off to a remote wood somewhere so no one could disturb them while he embarked on whatever manner of assault he had planned? On the other hand, she'd promised to make herself available for his questions. She could hardly refuse every suggestion he made simply because she couldn't seem to keep her senses in check when she was around him. Just the same, he might have worn a pair of jeans that didn't emphasize his male parts with such enthusiasm.

"Okay," she agreed finally. "Shall I change my clothes?"

She knew her appearance hadn't escaped his notice. Even so, he seized the excuse she'd handed him to give her plain cotton blouse and circular skirt a thorough inspection.

She wasn't quite sure what he found so intriguing about the way she looked. She barely thought beyond modesty in the style of her clothes and makeup. She couldn't help it if, without her attention to it, the material of even a simple costume like this conformed to the fullness of her breasts and followed the curves of her slim waist and hips. Her long red-gold tresses, confined today in a loose braid and tied with a yellow ribbon to match her costume, hung over one shoulder with provocative abandon. But none of this resulted from any deliberate effort.

She opened her mouth for the purpose of jostling his attention back to the question that had provoked all this scrutiny when he spoke up.

"Don't-just the way you are is fine," he said, clearing his throat. "If we should run into any brambles," he wiggled his eyebrows and flexed his fingers like the cunning rogue in an old melodrama, "I'll think of some way to handle the situation."

Still reluctant to risk a suggestive retort, she said nothing. But she couldn't help smiling at the lightness of his remarks and his mood. Was he trying to make her forget the dangers he posed? Was she that afraid to be alone with him in some secluded place?

Once before, she'd been enticed to a remote spot by a man whose danger she had ignored—with devastating results.

"All right then, I guess I'm ready." That winning smile of his overcoming her fears, she laughed and accepted his outstretched hand.

Despite continued feelings of inadequacy about her sexual sophistication, Jade realized she'd gained a measure of competence at normal conversation with Cain. She became aware of this change a few minutes later on the road traveling toward his property. His innate virility (rendered even more potent by their closeness inside the Jeep) never strayed far from her conscious thought. Nevertheless, the respect she had commanded during the past few days because of her professional abilities had bolstered her confidence to participate in a companionable exchange.

"Your choice of vehicles interests me," she said when the Jeep bounced over a rough spot on the highway. "I never quite pictured you in a Jeep."

He glanced at her and chuckled. "The ride too rough for you?"

She smiled back. "No way. I love the way these things handle."

"So do I," he said. "My work at the gallery takes me to a lot of out-of-the-way places. Artists can live in some peculiar locations. I trust this baby," he patted the steering wheel, "to get me where I'm going and back." He glanced meaningfully at her. "But you sound like you've driven a Jeep before?"

"You bet I have." She laughed with remembrance. "My friends and I used to rent one to take into the mountains when we had a holiday from school. You need a vehicle that responds well on those country roads in Europe. You have to keep your wits about you, too. I was always the driver everybody trusted." Her smile turned mischievous.

"But the way I rounded those curves, I'd have probably scared you to death."

"Maybe you'd like to drive on the way back" he offered, grinning back at her. "You won't scare me. At least your driving won't." His expression sobered slightly as he muttered the enigmatic addendum.

"We'll just have to see, won't we?" she said, the full meaning of her reply equally obscure in her own mind. Then, without thinking, she added, "Maybe I can find out whether you're as tough as you'd have me believe."

As so often before, she had the urge to grab back her last remark, but she relaxed when his wide grin indicated he hadn't read anything into it.

Her attention drawn to the view out the window, Jade gazed upon seas of pine forests with little ships of hardwood, banners waving with intense autumn color, anchored randomly throughout. Occasionally, a patchwork island of cultivated farmland or grassy tract of pasture broke into the continuum. Anyone from around here could tell you the Blue Ridge country ranked second only to Washington state in volume of timber. She would add that Georgia's forests furnished a lot of beauty to the countryside, as well.

After miles of winding highway, the Jeep handled just as easily on the gravel road Cain turned onto a half hour later.

"We're nearly there," he said, confirming her guess that they were now headed toward his property. "The timber man I told you about said he'd meet us at the southeast corner of my parcel. There's a thick stand of pine trees right around there."

Cain had barely spoken before she spotted a dark blue pickup pulled off to the side of the road. The name *Scott and Sons Lumber Company* was emblazoned across the door. As they pulled in behind the truck, a tall, wiry man dressed in faded jeans and a checkered shirt stepped out of it and waved a greeting.

Clearly an outdoorsman, his skin had acquired that ruddy leathered look inevitable after repeated exposure to the sun. A bill cap with his company logo stamped on it perched on top of a shock of fiery red locks that looked in need of a haircut.

"Mighty nice of y'all to drive all the way out here," he hollered, breaking into a wide, toothy grin as Cain opened his door and stepped out of the Jeep. He had barely closed the door before the stranger grabbed his hand and began to pump it vigorously.

"Good to see you again, Mr. Delancy."

"How are you, Mr. Scott?" Cain acknowledged, then, retrieving his hand, he turned to open the passenger door. His introduction of Jade prompted another enthusiastic smile from the lumberman and a sincere though gentler handshake.

"Glad you came along, ma'am," he said, withdrawing his callused appendage from hers. "My wife will appreciate having another woman to keep her company." He turned and hailed toward the pickup. A slight woman with freckled cheeks framed by a wad of pale yellow curls emerged carrying a baby in her arms. “Come on over here, honey,” he encouraged, “I want you to meet this lady.”

Looping one long arm around her shoulders, “This is my wife, Carol Ann,” he said. The woman nodded a shy smile in their direction, but said nothing. “And this here,” he reached out his rough hand with infinite gentleness, barely touching the delicate cap of almost white hair on the infant’s head, “this is our boy, Jimmy Junior.” The loving look in his eyes skittered from the baby back to its mother. “Mighty proud of this family of mine.”

The two men exchanged a few words relating to the business that had brought them here, then Cain suggested they walk over to take a look at the stand of pines Jim had in mind to purchase.

“Ma’am, don’t take offense at Carol Ann’s quiet,” Jim said to Jade when the men turned to leave. “Her deafness tends to make her standoffish with strangers.”

After the two males had disappeared into the woods, Jade ventured an encouraging smile at the other woman. Privately, she scolded herself for not recognizing the signs right away. She had observed the same reticence among deaf children during her volunteer work. Without the spoken word to depend on, a person must feel like a perpetual outsider. A man she knew with perfect hearing probably felt a similar detachment, albeit not in the same way.

“How old is your baby?” she ventured in sign language, choosing the subject she thought most likely to invite a response from the new mother.

At first, Carol Ann looked startled as Jade’s fingers plotted out the words. Then another more confident smile relaxed the other woman’s features. With amazing skill, considering she still cradled the baby firmly in her arms, she signed the reply, “Almost fourteen months.”

During the conversation that followed, Jade found Jim’s wife to be an amiable person who craved adult company as much as any new mother. Her husband worked long hours, and she’d obviously discovered that it required an enormous amount of energy to keep ahead of the miniature tornado she held in her arms. The baby, Jade learned, found new ways very day to wreak havoc on his environment. Apparently, his latest fascination was flushing his toys down the toilet.

As if starved for a place to invest her words, Carol Ann's flying fingers clicked off signs. Despite their fatiguing schedules, the Scotts seemed delighted with the addition of young Jimmy to their family. Jade asked who the boy favored, and that evolved into a discussion of the relatives and the lumber business that had been in the Scott family for generations. Jim's main worry seemed to be that he might fail to prove worthy of carrying on the family name. Jade could have told her companion she knew another son who felt the same inadequacy.

By the time the men emerged from among the trees, the two women had enjoyed a pleasant exchange. The males continued to discuss their business, and, knowing Carol Ann's arms must be tired by now, Jade offered to hold the baby.

Carol Ann hesitated at first, then smiled and handed the fidgeting bundle into her arms. Jade felt instant delight with the touch of the child's warm, tender skin. She understood now how great a blessing a baby must be to a family, and her mind toyed with the idea of having one of her own someday. A very pleasant thought, she decided, if she found the right man to become his father. Suddenly, instead of blue eyes and cotton white hair, her imagination substituted an image of dark eyes peeking from beneath silky brown ringlets. The picture vanished, however, as little Jimmy jerked her back from her musings with a healthy tug on her long braid of hair.

******

Cain had listened with interest to Jim Scott's plan to log his property. The lumberman's commitment to harvest the pines without disturbing the hardwoods impressed him. For some reason he couldn't define, he felt reluctant to desecrate this property. The two men had just stepped into the clearing where the women waited when another vision captured his attention.

It was one of those uniquely candid moments which seemed to accompany Jade's presence wherever she went. She stood cradling the towheaded infant in her arms as expertly as if she'd practiced with her own. Dressed in a simple cotton blouse and skirt and engaged in a conventional domestic task, nevertheless, she remained the most provocative woman he'd ever encountered. Even as his body reacted to her sensuality, an almost hypnotic force drew his eyes to that expressive face of hers. Spontaneous pleasure and tenderness clearly showed in her reactions. Some other not quite identifiable emotion played there, as well. Hope or anticipation perhaps?

This was a woman overdue for a sexual awakening. What a rare gift she would bestow on some lucky man when she gave herself completely. Partly out of selfishness, he felt glad that circumstances had interrupted her giving of that precious gift to a thief like Bonn Corbett. He would have considered her offering of no more consequence than a stolen moment to appease his sexual appetite. More than anything he'd ever desired, Cain hoped the next time Jade trusted enough to offer, she might choose him to receive the prize of intimate surrender.

Enmeshed in a web of musings woven around the scene in front of him, Cain had almost forgotten the other man.

"Sorry," he said, snatching his attention back to the present. "Sometimes I just can't help, well—"

"I don't blame you, man," Jim drawled with a knowing grin. "I do the same thing with Carol Ann, more than ever these days watching her with our baby. Just something about having a person so wonderful belong to you. And now with a family, too, you know, it overwhelms the senses sometimes." The man's ruddy complexion blazed with added color.

Unable to push words past the knot in his throat, Cain merely nodded. Suddenly, he envied everything this simple man had. Embarrassed, he looked away, only to have his gaze reclaimed by a pair of jade green eyes.

"Don't know how Ms. Hartman got Carol Ann to hand over that baby, though." Jim said, clearing his own throat. His eyes directed at his laughing wife, "Your lady must be something real special," he added.

"She certainly is," Cain agreed absently, his eyes still intent on the subject of their remarks.

A sixth sense lured Jade's attention from the infant she held in her arms to the two men. For seconds, her eyes locked with Cain's What she saw in those shadowed orbs she couldn't quite comprehend. That raw desire which always stirred her senses with equal measures of fear and attraction was certainly apparent. But something else touched her deeply, as well—an angry frustration shadowed by a despair so profound it made her want to reach out and rescue him.

The two men passed a few more minutes in discussion before they consented to a verbal contract. Agreeing on a time to meet to commit it to paper, they shook hands.

Carol Ann accepted her young charge from Jade with profound thanks for the respite and a smile that resounded her gratitude for the companionship of another woman.

"Pleasure doing business with you," Jim shouted out the window of his pickup as he pulled around the Jeep and drove away.

"Nice people," Jade said to Cain, oddly recalling she'd made the same comment recently about his parents.

"Yeah, having a family like that must be nice." His muttered response didn't quite conceal the trace of bitterness.

"Now then, let's see if we can find us a spot for that picnic," he said with obvious effort to stab energy into his voice. His look was still a little strange when he reached out his hand inviting her to come with him.

Jade hesitated. Had absence of opportunity or intention held Cain back from pressing intimacy during these last days? What was his real motive for bringing her out to this secluded property? For a second, she felt uneasy rumblings, then they settled without warning her off.

"I think we've both had time to work up an appetite by now," she said accepting his hand.

"I certainly have," he said lightly. Busy with surveying her surroundings, she didn't catch the darker affirmation in his eyes.

The picnic basket and a blanket in his free hand, he led her into a dense thicket of young trees. She hoped he didn't have much of a hike in mind. Even the sun couldn't reach into this undergrowth. However, they'd trekked only a short distance when the forest suddenly thinned into a clearing several acres in diameter. Except for a few oaks and poplars which formed a semicircle around a peculiarly level knoll, only grass and wildflowers populated the hidden pasture.

A small creek ribboned around the edge of the knoll. There beneath one of the huge oak trees Cain halted. "Right here's a good spot, I think." When Jade smiled in agreement, he set down the picnic basket, then, letting go of her hand, he stooped to spread the blanket on the ground.

"Here, let me help with that." She dropped lightly onto her knees and the gathers of her skirt settled in a lazy pool around her. Opening the picnic basket, she began pulling out the contents and arranging them on the checkered cloth.

When, after several seconds, her companion had not joined her on the ground, she raised her head. He stood looking down at her, his features constricted in another curious expression.

"Cain, is something wrong?" she asked cautiously.

"You know, you make a picture no matter what you're doing," he said when she spoke his name again. His eyes remained intent upon her, as though she were an image he'd etched in his memory yet couldn't quite believe really existed.

"Not fair making me blush," she said, a little unnerved by the intensity of his gaze. "Red's not my best color. Come on, sit down," she urged, holding out her hand to him. "I'm ready for some food and you can tell me about this place while we eat." She glanced around. "It sort of reminds me of a place my mother spoke about visiting a long time ago."

For a millisecond, that dreaded shadow dragged across his countenance like a widow's veil. Then it wiped away and was replaced by his former jovial expression.

Crossing his legs Indian style, he dropped down lithely next to her on the blanket.

"Mmm, let's see what we have here," he drawled. With a cleverness at turning a moment's innocence to his advantage, he lifted her hand to his mouth and licked the tips of her fingers. "Fried chicken, one of my favorites."

Before she could decide whether she should have allowed his forward gesture, he gave her back her hand. He didn't follow up on the intimacy, and she told herself she was glad. Pretending she attached no more importance to it than he did, instead, she prompted him with casual questions about his property and he seemed to accept the diversion.

"How big is this whole property?" she asked.

"As timber country is measured, not big enough to make me rich," he explained.

"Ever thought about building a house out here?"

"No, never," he said a little too vehemently. "I sell some of the timber from time to time, but I've never considered any other use for it."

If he had no real plans for the land, Jade wondered, why didn't he just sell it? But the choices he made for his life were really not her business. She decided just to enjoy the fresh air and the food in companionable silence. The housekeeper had prepared a feast of flaky fried chicken and several side dishes. She'd even tucked in little frosted cakes for dessert. Finally, after they'd exhausted the last of the goodies, they lingered awhile over a second glass of wine.

"You still curious about this place?" Cain spoke up, interrupting her contemplative gaze at the barren knoll.

She turned toward him and set her glass aside. "I can't help wondering," she admitted, "why did you buy a piece of land this far out in the first place?"

"I didn't buy it. Cy and Leona gave it to me. They called it my coming-of-age present when I turned twenty-one. More than once I've thought about selling it to pay for a gallery of my own since they're probably never going to turn theirs over to me. But somehow, I've never felt quite right about letting it go."

Jade nodded, though she still didn't understand, at all. Strange, how generous the Larkins had behaved at times, yet they remained so stubborn about giving their foster son what he truly wanted.

"I was thinking there might have been a house on that knoll at one time," she speculated, "or maybe a hunting lodge?" Her mother's reminiscences about a property just like this had included a description of a quaint little cabin with a stone chimney.

He shrugged. "Looks like it's been leveled off for some reason, doesn't it?"

"You don't know?"

He shook his head. "If there had once been a structure of some kind there, nothing was left of it when I received the land." A sudden furrow plowed deep into his brow as he turned his head and stared off in the direction she'd pointed. "Maybe that's it, the reason I've never been able to sell the place. There has always been something oddly familiar about it..." His remark seemed a thought unwittingly spoken aloud.

Jade had the same feeling about their surroundings. However, she knew her sense of *deja vu* likely resulted from her mother's stories about the place she'd visited as a young woman.

"Maybe someone brought you here a long time ago," Jade suggested, "when you were a child."

He blinked and pulled his attention back to her. "Yeah, could be that's it. But I don't remember ever coming here. I'm pretty sure Cy and Leona never brought me."

"How did they get the land?"

"Leona claims it was a legacy from her father," he said.

"Don't you believe her?" Jade asked, noting his skeptical tone.

His lips curled into one of those unsettling, humorless smiles. "I tend to question a lot of things Cy and Leona say and do, haven't you noticed?"

"Surely you can't really question that they love you?" came to her lips in automatic response.

A hollow chuckle rumbled in this throat. "I'm not even sure I believe in love."

Jade found his blatant assessment sad and somehow disconcerting. "How about the kind of love that happens between a man and a woman?" she found herself asking. "I admit, I'm an amateur about the mechanics of it. But I know one thing. Love has to be the focus of any relationship or it doesn't mean a thing."

The edge of his mouth curved, this time in a slightly teasing grin. "Maybe you could teach me about love." He reached out and trailed his finger down her cheek in a gentle caress. "And, in return, I could teach you some of the mechanics."

"No! You don't think—? I mean I wasn't asking—" Fumbling for words, she jerked away. "I'm sorry. Please don't get the wrong idea. I never meant to suggest—I'm sorry," she repeated, unable to prevent the desperation in her voice.

"Whoa, hey, relax." As if he expected a continued barrage of verbal reprimands, Cain held up his palms in a gesture of defense. "I never thought anything like that, I assure you."

"Sorry," she said again. "I guess I can't help being touchy about sexual innuendos." Self-censure cut into her tone.

"Because of what that bastard Corbett did to you?" he asked.

"More because of what I did to him."

That reply clearly caught Cain off guard. He stared at her from beneath drawn eyebrows. "What could you have done to him that he didn't deserve at least ten-fold?"

She sighed heavily. More of her naivete revealed, she thought dejectedly, but how could she take it back it now? Her remark had opened the door.

"You said you hadn't seen anything in the papers about Bonn's arrest?" she began.

"No, I must have missed it."

"It all came unraveled a little more than a month ago. With most stories like that, the media would have milked it forever."

He shrugged. "I never saw anything about it that I can recall. Like I told you, I've been out of the country a lot this spring. I guess the whole thing must have blown over before I got back from Europe."

She nodded. "That could be. The media did quiet down about it sooner than I expected. Maybe they decided the public was bored with stories about corrupt people in Washington. You can bet the rag sheets would still be splashing it across the headlines, though, if their reporters had gotten hold of my name. The colonel used the last bit of influence he had to keep that from happening."

"He cared what happened to you?" Cain inserted.

"Oh, no, he did it to protect his daughter. My entrance into the picture would have opened up a whole new scandal about Bonn's sexual escapades."

"Well, at least you got one break in that whole mess," Cain said sympathetically. "You might have had every rag sheet in the country holding you up for public view."

"Yes, I did escape that," she murmured, then continued in a louder tone, "I didn't get off scot-free, though. When Bonn's wife said her piece in my office, one of the things that angered her was having to keep silent about me to avoid more scandal. She'd convinced herself that her husband's downfall was my fault. She claimed I knew he was weak and I took advantage of it. If I'd left him alone, she said, none of the rest of it would have happened."

"You shouldn't have paid any attention to her," Cain argued gently. "Plainly, she was out of her mind with grief."

When after several seconds Jade hadn't said anything, "Even so, you feel guilty about that, too, don't you?" he asked, as though another glimmer of understanding had shone through. "You wonder if what she said was true, that you did set the whole chain of events into motion?"

"Yes," Jade admitted almost in a whisper.

"Now the painting has shown up like some kind of public denouncement?"

She nodded.

"Good Lord, how can you even allow thoughts like that into your head?" The soothing stroke of his voice defied the gruffness of his words. "I don't think you'd know how to lead a man on. It certainly never crossed my mind a few minutes ago that you intended anything like that. I do think you were duped by a philandering bastard who took advantage of your honest feelings and meant to use you to accomplish whatever dishonest scheme he had planned.

"I won't take advantage, though," he said, holding her steady in his gaze. "I won't take anything for granted, either. Nothing will happen between us unless we both want it to happen, I promise you, Jade." He paused, then added, "Will you trust me that far?"

She stared into the dark caverns of his eyes, still a little unsettled, but no longer fearful.

"Yes," she said with breathless certainty. It was she who reached out this time.

Her small hands caressed the slight roughness of his cheek. He lifted her wrists to his lips and feathered kisses into each of her palms. His gaze still unflinching, he guided her hands to rest on his shoulders, then let his own hands drop to his sides.

Jade felt no urge to pull away. Quite the contrary, her fingers tingled with eagerness to pursue the adventure. Free to seek their own response, her small hands glided around her partner's neck and burrowed into his thick, dark curls. She stared into the face now only inches from her own; she'd never looked at a man this close before.

During the few kisses she'd received from youthful suitors, her eyes had fluttered shut before the closeness progressed this far. Bonn's kisses had been so calculated, she'd barely had time to part her lips before he moved to conquer them.

She found this teasing intimacy fascinating, exhilarating, almost magnetic. Her lips ached for the touch of Cain's, so much that, reflexively, she pushed out the bud of her tongue to moisten the starved cushions of flesh.

Her partner could hardly have missed the signals her body transmitted. Nevertheless, he held off any active response. Only his hooded eyes betrayed the intensity of his desire as he permitted her to play out her senses.

The absence of threat in his technique was itself seductive, Jade realized. At the same time, it furnished her with enough confidence to surrender to her passion. Her movements like the rippling of silk, she closed the space between them and let her eyelids drift languidly over the jade treasures beneath.

Accepting his cue at last, Cain joined in his own seduction. He guided his lips with flawless precision to mesh with the softness of hers. She jerked her mouth slightly away, then relaxed into the pleasant joining of flesh.

At first, only their lips participated in the gentle rocking massage. But when the tightening of Jade's fingers in his hair signaled her need for more, Cain lifted his hands, sliding them around her waist to pull her closer.

She didn't resist at all this time. Instead, an intense need prompted her to step up her pursuit. As his arms wrapped around her, she relaxed the soft curves of her body into the hard planes of his. Her breasts squeezed against the taut muscles of his chest, and the heat from their bodies combined in scorching communion. Even the feel of his male member hard against her hips did not cool her ardor. Atop twin mounds of hot flesh, her nipples peaked tightly against the fragile fabric of her blouse.

By this time, Jade had evolved from the cautious pursuer into the bold aggressor, and her partner had become a willing accomplice. She plowed frenzied fingers into his hair and tore at his shirt in a frustrated need to bring him even closer. Their mouths became voracious takers in a blood pounding urgency to appease their carnal appetites.

Then, without warning, Cain changed to a message of retreat. The pressure of his lips ebbed away. A second later, he loosed his arms from around her waist and shifted out of her grasp. Her eyelids fluttered, then jerked open in a confused stare.

"I want you to let me do that again," he managed through labored swallows of breath.

"What?" she whispered between her own desperate gasps for air.

"Honey, if I don't back off," he said, then had to swallow hard again before he could continue, "well, let's just say I'm already having a hell of a time hanging on to any kind of control.

"I want to taste a lot more of you, but you need time to think about what you're getting into. I don't want to scare you off, but if I don't pull away right now, I can't answer for what might happen." He uttered a shaky chuckle. "You have no idea what you do to me, Jade Hartman."

"No, I guess I don't," she said, catching on finally. "I realize I'm not very skilled at this. I-I'm grateful to you for stopping before I made a complete fool of myself." Too embarrassed to meet his gaze any longer, she lowered her eyelashes.

"Jade, no, look at me." He reached out again and framed her face inside his long fingers. His hands felt warm and strong and gentle, like a breeze that carries a faltering ship to safe harbor. Dark earth reclaimed translucent jade as she raised her eyes to stare back at him.

"Listen to me, Jade," he urged. "You are good at this. Too good, that's the problem. I'm not talking skill; I'm talking honesty. Your feelings are all right there in your face. It's the most powerful aphrodisiac I've ever encountered. And I'm as susceptible as any other man. At this moment, I'd like nothing better than to lay you down right here in this field of flowers and make love to every inch of that luscious body.

"But I won't," he was quick to reassure when a shudder trembled through her limbs. "We'll take things slowly. When you're ready to give yourself to me, you'll let me know. Then it'll be right for both of us." The pressure of his fingers against her cheeks increased ever so gently. "Okay?"

Uncertain of what exactly she had assented, nevertheless, she nodded. She agreed that they should take things slowly. (Thank goodness, Cain had had the presence of mind to rein in his appetites before her reckless senses broke away completely from her judgment.) But did she agree with his prediction that they would eventually make love?

"Want to walk along the stream a little?" he asked. The steadiness of his speech indicated he'd regained control of his desire. "I think we both need to work off a little pent-up energy."

His insinuative chuckle brought fresh color to Jade's cheeks. However, she detected none of the old mocking, and she felt safe enough to respond with a tentative smile.

Her eyes followed the small trough of glassy water meandering along the edge of the clearing until it disappeared into a cluster of trees.

Strangled out by the dense shade, vegetation alongside the creek bank dwindled to a few ferns and brave sprigs of grass.

The uneven ground his excuse this time, Cain caught hold of Jade's hand. She might have told him she didn't require his assistance. Though her canvas espadrilles scarcely qualified as hiking shoes, she'd earned enough experience in the rugged hills near her home to manage this bit of rough terrain. Nevertheless, she condoned his ploy, even aided it by lacing her fingers with his.

Cain didn't press conversation with the woman walking at his side. For one thing, like Jim Scott with his wife and child earlier, he enjoyed just watching her every movement. She paused now and then to touch a flower or gaze at some small woodland creature occupied with its daily foraging. Every minute stroke of nature's artistry seemed to excite her with the wonder of an innocent seeing it for the first time.

Another preoccupation accounted mainly for his silence, though. The more he tried to assess the contradictions of his feelings, the more frustrating they became. He'd begun to care very much for this living image of the face on a canvas. Yet he had to have answers to some questions—even if it meant using her to get them.

At that moment, nature interrupted with another detour into the magic that seemed a part of Jade's presence. Without warning, a doe almost full grown, her coat shiny as brushed velvet, appeared at the stream only a few feet away. Cain stopped dead in his tracks, but the sight seemed to entice Jade to venture closer. She slipped her hand from his and moved forward in slow, measured steps. The doe hadn't seen either of them yet, and they remained downwind of her. The timid creature began to drink from the cool water, oblivious of the human stalkers nearby.

With her usual silkiness of motion, Jade sank onto one knee and contemplated the phenomenon in mute appreciation. Certain that the animal would sense their presence at any second and bound away, Cain raised the camera slung around his neck. He had to have this photograph. The child-woman, her face still flushed with the latent embers of passion, gazing wonderingly upon this delicate woodland creature; it was an opportunity every dedicated photographer prayed he might encounter.

Then something struck Cain like Fate sounding an alert—the resemblance. Jade's pose matched that of the woman in the painting! Even the background looked identical.

Who *are* you, Jade Hartman? he mouthed silently.

In almost simultaneous reactions, he clicked the shutter of the camera and the deer jerked her head up and vaulted away into the forest. Jade shifted her gaze in his direction and smiled. His mind boggled by the wealth of feeling in every one of her responses, his fingers reflexively clicked the camera one more time.

Was he anything like the other man who'd become so enamored of that face? Cain had to wonder. At first, he'd thought his own attraction had evolved out of obsession with the painting. But he knew now that the truth lay deeper than a two-dimensional portrait. Not a face on canvas, but Jade herself, had gotten into his blood.

He hadn't reckoned on holding onto her for more than a brief space of time. He'd enjoy her company for a few days while he prompted her to share information about her family (her mother, in particular). Perhaps during that interval, she'd permit him to experience the total wonder of her with a few passionate nights of lovemaking. But he'd never imagined he could entice her to stay longer—especially if he revealed what he intended to do with some of the snapshots he'd taken today.

Now Fate had tricked him again. A simple attraction had increased into a desperate need to have her. Not for a few days, but forever. She was no longer just a face that duplicated the one in the portrait. She'd become a real woman to him, and he wanted everything that real woman offered.

How could he make her stay, though? Up to now, he'd depended upon the assistance of circumstances to hold her in Atlanta. But he must provide her with a reason to remain permanently. Given time, he might make her understand the motives behind his deceptions and persuade her to stay permanently with him, as well.

CHAPTER SIX

"If this is a family thing, wouldn't I be intruding?"

"Nonsense, my dear," Leona said, again pressing her invitation for Jade to share the social evening she had planned. "You wouldn't be intruding, at all. Professor Collier is merely an old friend we often invite to join us for dinner. We want you to be there. I'm sure Lawrence would enjoy meeting you."

Cain's foster mother had stopped in at the cottage to see if her guest needed anything, a routine she had repeated several times during these past few days. While Leona rattled off the credentials of the other guest they had invited for dinner this evening, Jade thought about how fond she'd become of both the Larkins. Cain's foster parents seemed, in every sense, warm and loving people.

Which made it even more difficult to figure out why they might have refused to take steps to make Cain their son.

"It was Cain's suggestion," Leona explained. "That we invite Lawrence over so we could ask his opinion on several pieces of Chinese art we've been thinking about purchasing for resale. I decided to turn our meeting into a social occasion. We all enjoy Lawrence's company. And I didn't think you'd mind a new face at the table."

"Of course I don't mind," Jade assured her.

Maybe Leona Larkin didn't have any choice in the matter of Cain's adoption, Jade speculated, still distracted about the possible motive for what seemed a cruel omission.

Could Cy have some hang-up about lending his name to an orphan? Or perhaps he was a bit of a genealogical snob, and something related to Cain's birth family offended his pedigree. On occasion, she still glimpsed a wariness in the older man's eyes when she mentioned her own parents.

"Professor Collier has offered us his expert advice on a number of occasions," Leona went on in her explanation. "He's been a good personal friend, as well. I'm sure you'll like him."

"I'm sure I will, too," Jade agreed. "Thank you for including me in your evening, Leona. I'll try to find something special to wear."

"Oh, my dear girl," the other woman said, clucking her tongue. "What you wear isn't really important. You're a beautiful young woman. I only mentioned our guest because I wanted to fill you in on what to expect this evening."

After a farewell full of good spirits, Leona took her leave. She never stayed long, Jade noticed. Sometimes it seemed as if she actually feared Cain might catch her there.

Jade appreciated the special dinner invitation. Nevertheless, she wondered if perhaps Cain's foster mother had urged her to be present because Leona knew if Jade agreed to come to dinner, her son would come, as well. Leona had called Lawrence Collier a friend of the family. Did that include Cain? Maybe he never felt obliged to attend a social evening with the Larkins unless given some particular reason.

Whatever Cain might lack in cordiality where his foster parents were concerned, Jade couldn't fault his graciousness toward her during the time she'd spent in Atlanta.

With his business concluded a few days ago, Mr. Muhaffa had departed with an acceptable increase to his fortune and a considerable boost to the harmony of his household. Jade realized she was in some small way responsible for both changes. And the African had finally acknowledged her assistance with a few words of thanks. He hadn't even seemed to mind that her fashion advice to his newest wife had cost him a sizable portion of the bank draft he'd received from the Larkins.

Using the reasonable argument that she owed herself another vacation after her stressful occupation with the African entourage, Cain had persuaded Jade to stay awhile longer in the city.

When the two of them went out together (he'd treated her to some of the most elegant dining experiences Atlanta had to offer) he always showed her marked attention. True to his promise, however, he had not pressured her toward intimacy. His kisses were warm and frequent, but unaggressive. She couldn't tell yet whether he had any feelings for her deeper than lust (despite a poverty of experience, even she could tell his restraint was costing him). Though that uneasy shadow still passed over his countenance from time to time, he did seem more accepting of the fact that she wasn't hiding information about her family.

On several occasions, he'd encouraged her to share anything she might remember about the stories her mother told her. That is, until a few days ago when he seemed to have heard something that appeased his curiosity. The scene was still vivid in her memory.

"I understood you to say you don't look anything like your mother?" Cain questioned when Jade made yet another reference to her parents. "Do you happen to have a picture of her with you?"

"Of course, I always carry one." She reached for her purse and drew out the snapshot. She smiled at the solemn face in the photo, then handed it to Cain. He studied the picture for minutes before he returned it to her.

Disappointment clear in his features, "Your mother's hair seems to have turned white early," he commented. "And pulled back that way, it's hard to tell if it's curly."

"Actually, it's looked that way as long as I can remember," Jade explained. "She suffered a serious accident many years ago. I understand trauma can turn a person's hair white prematurely. If you just consider her facial features, though, you can see we don't look much alike."

"No, you don't," he agreed. "I sense a resemblance, but your mother shouldn't have changed that much in twenty-five years. She does have those same telling eyes. I wonder..." His voice trailed off as though he were considering something, then he shook his head. After a moment, he seemed to return to her, and before she could question what he might have been thinking, he let out a long sigh and reached to gather her into his arms. For minutes more, he merely held her in silence, and by then she was too confused to pursue the matter any further.

She did notice he hadn't asked anything more about her family since that time.

While the aforementioned events had played out, their personal attraction had intensified—to such a degree that Jade had come to believe Cain might have been right in his prediction about their eventual intimacy. Though he'd held to his promise not to press her, she witnessed barely restrained lust in his countenance each time he let her go. Likewise, he had to have noticed signs of the tempest building inside her own breast.

Their passion too ravenous to be appeased any longer with these mere samplings of intimacy, it was inevitable that they would resolve their need in some way before she departed Atlanta.

Adding to her personal turmoil, she struggled to assign a name to the feelings she had for this dark man. Was it merely an overpowering lust that must be sated? No, it had to be more than that, she'd finally concluded. She still hesitated to use the word, "love." After all, she'd been too quick to affix that label to her relationship with another man—and still suffered from the disaster it had birthed.

She felt an equal uncertainty about Cain's response if she did venture her whole heart. Was he ready for any kind of permanent commitment? He wanted her, perhaps had even come to need her a little. But could he untangle his emotional bonds enough to give back love?

Whatever happened, it must be soon.

"I can't afford to vacation much longer," she'd already told Cain. "I have to give my answer about the embassy job in New York before it's filled." She'd agreed to stay through the weekend, but there could be no more delays. In two days, she'd be on a plane to Washington to begin reorganizing her life.

When Jade spoke to Cain about Leona's special invitation to dinner that evening, she was met with the first of several surprises from Cain.

"Of course I don't mind if we join Cy and Leona in entertaining Lawrence," he said, delivering the first surprise. "Actually, I'm looking forward to the evening."

His eager acquiescence had only been the start; as the evening progressed, his behavior boggled even more.

"Jade is as tasteful and elegant as you are, Leona," he announced to the entire gathering. Then, "Don't you think so, Lawrence?" he put to their guest.

For the occasion, Jade had subdued her mass of red-gold hair into a demure chignon. A simple collar necklace and slave bracelet supplied the only accents to her gold sheath dress. She already knew Cain appreciated the simple elegance of her costume, but she hadn't expected his unabashed praise in front of the older people.

"Like your mother, your young lady exhibits elegance along with beauty," Professor Collier agreed gallantly.

Jade barely had time to take in this blatant flattery before Cain followed with another reversal of any behavior she'd formerly witnessed in front of his family. A charismatic host replaced the subdued watcher who'd sat across from her through so many meals at his parents home. He seemed to consider it his pleasant duty to entertain both guests in the house. More to the point, he actually took pains to acquaint them with each other's interests.

Not that Jade actually minded Cain's openness. It encouraged everyone to speak more. Lawrence Collier was an interesting person and a skilled conversationalist.

Plainly, he was a gentleman of fastidious habits who had taken excellent care of his sixtyish physique. The precise grooming of his graying hair and mustache reminded her of Agatha Christie's fictional detective, Hercule Poirot. The professor held the prestigious position of Chairman of the Fine Arts Department at the University. According to what Cain had said earlier, he was an expert in Oriental art who enjoyed a reputation as a consultant for collectors all over the world.

"How many Eastern languages do you speak?" he elicited from Jade while their coffee was being served on the veranda. Earlier, Cain had lauded her contribution as interpreter for the African delegation. She'd just confided to Professor Collier that she had lived in Japan for a brief time when she was a child. She remembered her fascination with the land and its people. While her father had been often occupied with his study of ancient Japanese remedies for the treatment of burn victims, her mother had made it her project to teach both herself and her daughter the difficult Oriental language.

"I've acquired a good command of three standard dialects," she explained now to answer the professor's question, "but I have a fair speaking knowledge of several more."

She reeled off the Asian languages in her repertoire, and the academic seemed more than politely impressed. He fingered his immaculately barbered chin thoughtfully for a moment. "Jonas Barnes is Chairman of the Humanities Department at the University," he said finally. "He was telling me recently about the need for instructors in Eastern languages, especially Russian and Japanese."

When he looked at her as though he expected some reply, she reacted with a short laugh. "Professor, that's very interesting but I don't see what it has to do with me. I've never thought about teaching at a university."

"Oh, my dear," he said at once, "considering the extent of your talent, I had in mind something else entirely. I was thinking about a job in industry. As you must know, much of our country's business involves the Japanese these days. And with this fresh interest in Russian resources, bigger companies are anxious for their executives to learn the languages.

Only recently, I was told about two inquiries at the University for interpreters skilled enough in languages to teach classes and also provide translations during business meetings. Dr. Barnes, the man I mentioned, was lamenting the fact that he didn't have any graduates available at the moment who possessed such skills." Professor Collier lifted a card from his breast pocket and scribbled a name and number on the back. "Why don't you give Jonas a call," he said, holding out the card to her. "I'm sure he'd be eager to talk to you about this."

The almost perfect arches of Jade's eyebrows pinched into a frown. She glanced at Cain. He hadn't commented during this latest exchange, but he eyed her curiously, as though her response were of more than casual interest.

"I appreciate your gesture, Professor Collier," she said, turning toward him a more softened expression, "but I already have a job."

The academic darted confused eyes in Cain's direction. "Oh, oh, I see," he said, his confident speech showing a marked falter, "that is, I understood you were seeking employment here in Atlanta."

"I wonder how you got that idea," she said, shifting upon Cain another suspicious frown.

"Oh, well, ah—" The older man's former impeccable demeanor now resembled that of a clumsy swimmer who'd ventured too far into deep water. "Take the card anyway, Miss Hartman," he managed finally. "You might change your mind."

The dictates of good manners prompted Jade to accept the card from the hapless man's hand. After all, he wasn't the one who deserved to be left dangling.

Personifying the discreetly attentive hostess up to now, it was Leona who spoke up to rescue her guest from the awkwardness of the moment. "I hope you young people don't mind if I spirit the professor away. Cy and I want to get his advice on those oriental pieces we're thinking of bidding on before he has to leave."

"Oh, you're quite right, Leona." Professor Collier used the excuse of looking at his watch to clear his throat profusely. More in command of his voice, he continued, "We do need to get on with our business. So nice to have visited with you, young lady," he added, turning back to Jade. "I hope I have the pleasure again soon."

Like a seasoned actress about to cancel future performances, Jade spoke her farewells with gracious pretense to the company around her. Only when she and Cain were left alone did she bring the curtain down with a resounding thud.

"You're responsible for this, aren't you?" she blasted, marching forward to stand directly in front of Cain. She speared him with a look flaming with emerald fire.

"Jade, I didn't—" he started but she cut him off with, "What makes you think you have the right to arrange my life for me? Has everything that's happened these past weeks been manipulated by you to keep me here? I wonder now whether I've had any control over my life since the day I walked into your gallery."

She didn't wait for any more of his attempts at response. Unable to bear hearing another of Cain's trespasses cleverly justified, she turned on her heel and dashed out the French doors. Oblivious of the repeated calling of her name and even to the natural gifts proffered by the blissful summer evening, she pushed aside a shrub filled with fragrant blossoms and dashed across the lawn. Pausing only to slip off her strappy high heels, she crossed the new-mown grass to her cottage. Only when she reached the door to her quarters did she slow her steps. Suddenly drained of energy, she leaned a moment against the oak barrier.

"Damn the man!" she cursed into the quiet night. "How could he do this to me!"

From the time she'd unwisely barged into Cain Delancy's office, he had schemed to take control of her life. He'd finagled to keep her here weeks longer than she'd intended and, in the process, he'd gotten her to offer on her own exactly what he wanted.

And he'd done it all with such clever charm he had made her fall in love with him. There! she'd finally labeled it. Why had she thought she could avoid the feeling simply by refusing to give it its proper name? Even as she rejected the possibility of their having any future together, love was what she'd come to feel for this secretive stranger.

And what was worse, hope had crept in that she might have sparked a similar feeling in him. Now she'd had the truth hurled at her like a medicine ball to the gut. Cain didn't love her; he simply took some perverse pleasure in arranging her life. He was attracted to her on a physical level, and he needed time to set her up for the intimacy he was sure she would also volunteer. Producing temporary employment hadn't satisfied his plan, so he'd schemed to find her a more permanent situation.

"Damn!" she bit out again, this time in a frustrated whisper as she fumbled for the extra key she kept under the windowsill. "Why must I always get involved with men who want only to use me?"

Her hand finally closed around the key and, in one deliberate motion, she unlocked the door, slid through the opening and slammed it behind her. Her purpose already decided upon, she marched straight toward the bedroom. The strength of her muscles assisted by rage, she yanked her suitcases from a corner of the closet and flung them onto the bed. She'd barely emptied the first drawer into a case when she heard the front door bang open.

Like the crack of a rifle shot, a second later, the heavy barrier slammed shut again.

Poised for Cain's entry through her bedroom door, Jade whirled to face him, her eyes still spitting green fire.

"How dare you burst in here!" she hurled at him.

"It's my house!" he yelled, continuing to descend upon her.

"So it is," she said in a voice strained by rage. "And everything in it will be yours again as soon as I pack my things."

"You can't leave!" he said, as though he'd already made that decision for her, also. His determined strides halting within inches of her, he stood there glaring down into her fiery eyes. "I won't let you leave." The words came out in a scorching breath against her cheek, but she stood her ground.

"What's your latest maneuver to keep me here?" she demanded in a tone now filled with sarcastic ill-humor. "Guards at my door, perhaps?"

"If I have to," he snapped back at her.

She opened her mouth to deliver a blistering retort. Instead, her breath sucked in with a cry of astonishment when, as if he'd choreographed his motions, Cain swept the stack of suitcases from the bed and replaced them with their bodies. The next instant, he held her immobilized underneath the hard muscles of his chest. Her pitiful efforts to defend against his attack halted abruptly when his steel grip pinioned her arms above her head.

"You will not leave," he gritted through clenched teeth. Jade's wide-eyed stare ricocheted off the hard set of his mouth, only to crash into the same dark threat in his eyes. "I won't allow it, do you understand?"

"Let me go!" An icy blast of fear rippled through her body with the chilling realization of her vulnerability. Harboring no illusions about matching his physical strength, instead, she launched a renewed emotional attack. "You can't keep me here simply because it amuses you. I don't belong to you!"

"You think this roller coaster ride I've been on these past weeks amuses me?" His harsh laugh contained no trace of humor and his viselike grip betrayed no hint of mercy. "Hell, I've kept my hands off you longer than I ever have a woman. If all I wanted was to amuse myself, I could have taken you to bed days ago. But that's not what I want." She noted a slight softening in his tone. "What I want is you!"

The brutal frankness of his admission provoked a fresh shiver of fear. She'd been right a few minutes ago; he really wanted to possess her—like one of his paintings.

"You want me? What does that mean?" she questioned, dumbfounded. "You can't own people like works of art. I'm a person, Cain. I'm not that woman in the painting, you said so yourself. I'm a living, breathing human being, and you can't arrange my life so I'll be available whenever you *want* me for whatever your current entertainment might involve. You can't do that to me!" she squeezed out, as desperation threatened to topple her fortress of anger.

Jade thought she felt a slackening of his hold on her then, but the words he spoke made her certain she'd been mistaken.

"What I can't do is let you go."

She hadn't mistaken a similar note of desperation in his voice, though.

"I've helped you with your business deal and I've answered your questions," she reasoned with placating restraint. "You don't need me anymore. Why can't you just let me go?"

"Because-because I love you." The words wrenched from his lips in an agonized whisper.

She couldn't be wrong about the change in him this time. All the adrenalin-triggered fury seemed to drain from his body. His fingers relinquished their grip on her arms, and, a moment later, the weight of him ebbed away and he rolled onto the bed beside her.

One arm crooked so his eyes were shielded, he lay on his back next to her. For long minutes, he didn't speak. Finally, "I'm sorry I scared you," he said.

Pinioned now by the weight of astonishment, Jade found it impossible to move away. She sat up and rubbed her wrists to restore feeling. The last of the pins had been shaken from her hair, and her long mane cascaded over her shoulders like a waterfall flowing with pure gold.

More minutes ticked by while she sat there staring at the masked figure beside her. Had he meant the words of love he'd just spoken? As she'd loosed herself of the guilt which had hobbled her emotions for months now and allowed her senses the taste of real love, had he broken his own tether and rushed into the same tender fields? If it were true and he'd given in enough to his feelings to confess it, perhaps they had a chance for a future together, after all.

"Why did you try to arrange a job for me?" she asked aloud.

He didn't move. Again the quiet dragged on so long Jade thought he might not answer. Then, still with his eyes barricaded from her, he said, "I didn't. Lawrence reached that conclusion, I suppose, because I'd been checking about possible jobs with people at the University and any other contacts they referred me to. I meant to say something to you about it after the two of you had been introduced this evening. I thought he would be a good person to suggest more people you might contact. I guess he must have heard about my inquiries and taken it upon himself to keep an ear out."

"I see," she said quietly. "You should never have done any of those things, you know. It's my life and my future. You should have left me alone to make my own choices."

He sat up then, but he still seemed unable to look her in the eye. "I know what I did was out of line," he admitted, fixing his gaze upon the empty wall. "But I was desperate. I knew I was on borrowed time. You kept talking about leaving. I couldn't think of any other way to convince you to stay."

"Did you mean what you said?" she ventured. "That you love me?"

He turned finally to meet her gaze. "Yes, I love you," he said, and she saw truth behind the glaze of moisture in his earthlike eyes.

Her eyes bored into his with such intensity they might have reached into the rock that pocketed the gemstones they resembled. "Then why didn't you just ask me to stay?" she said at last.

A combination of surprise and elation vied for control in his features as he sprang to life. He reached out, but stopped short of touching her. "Would you-will you stay, Jade? God, I can't tell you how much I want that. Please say you'll stay-please."

She couldn't help a smile of amusement at Cain's uncharacteristic supplication.

"Yes, I'll stay—if I can find a job that suits me," she said, "but no more interfering in my life," she added in warning. "I found Professor Collier's suggestion interesting, and I'm definitely going to check it out. I'm going to search for any other possibilities, as well— on my own. If something looks promising, then we'll talk about whether I want to follow up on it But you stay out of it from now on," she added in another sober warning. She fixed him with a searching look. "Is that agreed?"

"Yes, agreed." His voice sounded husky with emotion, and his hand shook when he raised it to reaffirm his verbal promise.

Tentatively, he moved the same hand toward her close enough to touch a strand of her hair. "Like threads of spun gold," he murmured, looping the silken tress around his fingers. The shimmering mass plunged over her shoulders like Lady Godiva's dense tresses, swaddling her breasts in a vestment of gilt threads.

When Cain's gaze drifted back to meet hers, passion shadowed their dark earth tones. Not with the threat of minutes ago, but with the tortured hunger she'd seen there so often lately. For seconds, a silent message passed between them. Then, as though to banish his preoccupation, he shook his head and looked away.

"I'd better get out of here," he muttered. The barely audible declaration was laced with self-reproach. He swung his long legs off the opposite side of the bed and made to propel himself to his feet. But a small hand reached out to pull him back.

"No," Jade said simply when his attention snapped in her direction.

"Jade, please, I have to go," he said almost in a plea.

But her jade green eyes refused to surrender their hold on his deep brown ones.

"Why?" she asked in the same deliberate tone.

"For a lot of reasons," he said, again with gruff self-censure. "Because I didn't honor the promise I made to you. Because I lost control a few minutes ago and I might have hurt you. But mostly, because I want you right now more than is healthy for either of us."

He'd made it nearly to his feet when a soft, "No," trembled again from her lips.

For seconds, he seemed to freeze like a Greek statue. Then he sank back onto the bed. "Jade, listen to me," he implored in desperation, "you don't know what you're saying. If I stay now, I won't be able to stop—"

She pressed her fingers to his lips to halt his protest. "I know what I'm saying. I'm nervous and I'll probably disappoint both of us. But I know I want my first experience with love to be here and now—with you."

Though she'd granted him permission to touch her, still he hesitated. Hadn't he predicted they would make love when she was ready? Well, she was ready; her body language screamed it. Having admitted he loved her, did he now fear to give in to his feelings?

"Honey, think about this," he said. "Are you sure this is what you want? You might be making a worse mistake than before."

"I won't be making a mistake, not with you," she replied, now with absolute confidence. "I'm sure this time. Not in spite of what happened just now, but because of it. You couldn't hurt me then. And you won't hurt me now." She splayed slim fingers over his chest. "Please, Cain, stay."

The delicate touch of her flesh must have radiated a heat deep enough to reach his heart. Jade felt a shudder race through his body. Then, with a muffled groan, he released a long breath and gathered her into his arms.

CHAPTER SEVEN

"Easy, baby," Cain murmured. "Just take it slow. We have all the time the world. Just let it happen."

Cain's purring whisper was enough to convince Jade to submit to his superior skill at lovemaking. While she might have hurried the beautiful process like a clumsy innocent, instead, she allowed him to teach her the joys of a man and woman's intimate joining. He began with feathered kisses, so soft she barely felt his lips touch hers.

Finally, when he seemed satisfied that she trusted him, he covered her mouth with his and wrapped his arms around her. A second later, he moved so he lay facing her on the bed.

Through the fabric of his shirt, she felt the enticing heat of his body close to hers. A thrill of fear raced through her, yet, paradoxically, she had the strongest urge to move closer. At once, her body relaxed against his, molding each pliant curve against his taut muscles until she felt his hard arousal push into the flat surface of her stomach.

Jade couldn't remember exactly how her outer clothing disappeared from her body. She remembered only the feathery touch of skilled hands, then a delicious feeling as they glided over her naked flesh. A moment later, Cain slid away from her arms.

When she opened her eyes, he stood over her next to the bed. His bronzed body was covered only by a snug-fitting pair of blue boxers.

"Look at me, sweetheart," he whispered, unmoving. "If you want to stop now, tell me."

Embarrassed by the raw passion coursing through her veins, nevertheless, Jade did look. Her gaze snagged first on two dark eyes, hooded almost black now with desire as they bored into hers. Then she let her attention stray languidly downward. If Cain was worried that the sight of his nakedness might frighten her, he had no reason. The catch in her breath had nothing to do with fear.

His sheer maleness raised sensual longings more potent than a swami's hypnotizing music. Every nerve ending vibrated, as if a tuning fork had passed over it.

Her captured gaze followed the lean lines of his body from the dark patch of hair on his chest to where it narrowed into two symmetrical rows down his middle. His broad shouldered-physique was a blessing from the gods, for which, judging by their toned appearance, he showed his appreciation by working them out at a gym.

She knew she appreciated everything she saw. The moist heat converging in the lower regions of her own body told her so. The prospect of touching him, all of him, exhilarated her.

When her wanton eyes darted back to peer into his dark ones, she saw that concern now overlapped the heavy hood of desire. She shook her head in answer to his silent solicitation. No, she didn't want to stop. The power of her own feelings disturbed her a little. But she felt no fear of him.

Cain released his breath in a shaky sigh and nodded his understanding. Then, with one easy motion, he levered his body back onto the bed next to her. He was close enough to touch her, but he didn't. For seconds, he merely looked at her. The delicate wisps of flesh-colored silk and lace of her undergarments were almost camouflaged against her pale skin. His gaze intense enough to see right through them, clearly, he was struggling to keep his desire in check. Finally, he allowed his fingers the luxury of smoothing out her long hair, splaying the strands around her head like a sunburst of Aztec gold.

With the practiced restraint of one privileged to explore the timeless beauty of rare pieces of art, he glided his fingers over her bare shoulders and into the scoop of her neck.

"You're the most exquisite thing I've ever seen," he purred. "Jade." His mouth caressed her name with worshipful softness. A second later, his lips pressed against hers with the same profound adoration.

The feel of his exploring mouth had her so mesmerized she barely noticed as he slid her undergarments from her heated flesh. Only when his fingers touched her breasts did she become aware that she was totally naked. Her nipples hardened under his cupped hands, and her body arched in automatic reaction to his gentle massage.

Unsatisfied, his hands moved further down, his mouth following close behind with tender kisses. Conscious of her body as never before, she felt a flush of heat in her cheeks when his hands moved between her legs. Her lush eyelashes lowered in instant response.

But Cain wouldn't permit it. "Look at me, sweetheart," he said with gentle coaxing. "This is wonderful. You're wonderful—perfect." In his shadowed gaze, she saw desire tugging at his control. Yet even now, a generous buffing of adoration smoothed the roughness of his passion.

Encouraged to the point of boldness, suddenly, she wanted to touch him back.

She reached out, pushing trembling fingers into his dark mass of chest hair. She thrilled at his shivered response when her thumbnails grazed the small nipples. Prompted to further boldness, she laced her fingers around his neck and pulled him to her.

She had little knowledge about how a man proceeded with lovemaking, she realized, but she was enjoying her first lesson. His body, splayed partly on top of hers, felt warm and hard, and she understood at once how a man excites a woman's passion.

He was kissing her again, with more passion this time, his lips parting hers, his tongue reaching inside to caress the soft tissue there. And she was responding with her own passionate exploration.

The fire inside her burned so hot now she thought this must be the pinnacle of need when intimacy sought to achieve the ultimate joining. Why was Cain holding off? She was sure she was ready for him. Even so, she flinched in surprise when his fingers moved between her thighs again with lingering caresses that reached farther and farther inside, finally touching her woman's core.

"Shh," he soothed in a low whisper and she understood why he was holding off. "I want you to relax. Trust me. We'll get there soon."

And, under his gentle tutelage, she did relax. When the tenseness in her muscles released completely, she felt his fingers begin to move again inside her.

It was agonizing and wonderful at the same time. With every stroke she yearned for more. Her body was shaking with anticipation and when she thought she could take no more, Cain pulled away and stripped away the last of his clothing. While she stared for the first time at a man's full arousal, feeling more fascinated than afraid, he fumbled with a foil packet. Protection! Why had she not even thought of that until now? She *was* a novice at lovemaking. Perspiration beaded Cain's forehead by the time he had adjusted the shield over his sex. But even then he didn't move to satisfy his need. Instead, he searched her eyes one last time. In a tortured whisper, he spoke her name followed by the question, "Are you sure?"

Her need an undisputed match for his, she knew she didn't want to deny either of them, not now. "Please, Cain, yes," squeezed from her parched lips.

He nodded his understanding. Nevertheless, his eyes remained watchful as he eased himself between her thighs and touched his hardened member to her moist core.

Desperate to feel him inside her, she arched toward him.

"Slowly, baby," he whispered, "this may hurt a little." But a second later, he sank inside her.

It did hurt when her virgin shield tore apart, but the twinge was so fleeting she barely noticed. Then he was inside her fully, one with her, and ecstasy erased all pain and and fear. Intuition took over, and her body arched to encourage him to take everything he wanted. He hesitated an instant longer, then commenced a slow movement inside her.

All thoughts of pain disappeared inside a wonderful exhilaration, and she wanted him to take her completely, to exhaust them of all their energies, until they lay sated in each other's arms. Reacting to her encouragement, he moved with her, faster now, until she felt one final surge of sexual current race through her, then ebb away completely. A second later, her partner's body went rigid, then shuttered a terrific release of energy and finally relaxed against her.

His bronze skin glistened with perspiration and his breath pumped out in labored gasps. Their bodies remained joined, and there was something splendid during those seconds about just feeling him as one with her. Finally, he levered himself away, but even then, one arm held onto her in a tender embrace as he collapsed exhausted beside her.

"You okay?" he asked, still with an effort to slow his breath. "I didn't hurt you, did I?"

She reached out and touched his cheek. "I didn't know anything could feel so good."

One of those rare spontaneous grins she loved so much sprang to his lips. "It's never felt this good for me, I promise you."

"I didn't disappoint you, then. I mean, I don't know—"

"Jade," he interrupted, "my wonderful Jade, you've given me the most intense sexual experience I've ever had. I've been with lots of women so I do know. You offer yourself with absolute honesty; no experience is necessary for that, just true feelings."

His tone became peculiarly sober as he added, "All I'm thinking is I hope I'm worthy of the precious gift you've given me."

Then his eyes brightened and he chuckled. "And I'd like to think I'll get a lot more chances to appreciate you."

Hardly believing he hadn't read in her features the erotic thoughts which continued to tantalize her senses as their naked bodies caressed, she ventured, "Actually, I was hoping we might appreciate each other again right now. But maybe you need to rest awhile after…?" Her voice trailed off with a bashful grin.

Cain squeezed her tighter to him and she felt the hardness of his renewed arousal.

"Are you kidding, woman?" he said with mock gruffness. "Now that I've got you in bed finally, I have enough energy to do anything."

She laughed, but sobered immediately when her movement against his naked flesh triggered his instant arousal. More confident to express her own passion, she became an aggressive participant in this fresh round of lovemaking.

"Oh, baby, what you do to me," he murmured a second before she felt his hardened member sink inside her core again. There was no hesitation this time, only a ravishing hunger to satisfy their profound need. Their bodies trembled and climaxed almost simultaneously as the fires inside them burned themselves out.

"Forgive me, Jade," Cain murmured, then with a final exhausted sigh, he fell away from her. She wasn't sure what exactly he was asking forgiveness for—for taking her virginity, for making such passion-driven love that he might have hurt her, or for satisfying himself when he didn't feel worthy of her. But before she could ask, she heard his soft sighs fade into the steady breathing of deep sleep.

Well, they could talk later, she decided, snuggling closer to the warmth of the strong arm still draped across her hips. Exhilarated by the thought that, now that ain had declared his love, he would be here beside her when she awoke tomorrow morning and every morning thereafter, she smiled contentedly and closed her eyes.

"I want to wake up with you beside me like this every morning."

His body still damp from his recent shower, Cain tucked a towel around his waist and leaned over to kiss Jade's bare shoulder.

"I want that, too," she murmured to their reflections in the mirror. She stood with her hairbrush poised in mid-stroke, trying to assess Cain's meaning. Her terry robe hung loosely, barely covering the swell of her breasts which he seemed now intent upon caressing. Trying to hold onto her reason against the lure of his erotic touch, she stared at the glistening muscles of his bare torso. He was so gorgeous, so male, so everything she'd ever hoped for in a mate. Was his statement a hint that he wanted a permanent commitment? She knew already what her answer would be if he'd only get the words out.

Since their first night of lovemaking, all her dreams of a future had included Cain as her husband. Nevertheless, she hadn't allowed him to design a career for her. Determined that the self-approval she had attained of late should remain her master, she'd stuck to her insistence that Cain stay out of it. And he had.

She'd inquired about the position Professor Collier mentioned, of course. It was certainly intriguing and an avenue she'd never really explored. But she'd checked out other possibilities for employment, as well. In the end, she realized a job as a language instructor to adult professionals and interpreter for foreigner clientele suited her talents best and coincided with her resolution against dealing with political secrets.

When the personnel director of the largest international corporation in Atlanta had called back immediately to arrange a second interview, she realized how valuable her skills might be. An excellent job situation already secured, she was set to start her foreign language classes next week. Now all that remained to make her new life perfect was a marriage proposal from Cain.

"If you'd stayed at the cottage, we could have been together like this every night." he purred, dashing her hopes that marriage was what he intended to propose.

He knew already why she'd changed her living arrangements. As soon as she had a firm offer of a job, sending for her furniture and moving into her own apartment had been next on her agenda. She was not about to remain the Larkins' guest when she had her life set to move forward on her own again.

"I wouldn't have felt right about staying in the cottage, surely you see that?" she said to Cain, at the same time hoping her features didn't betray her disappointment that this was all he meant to talk about. "How would that have looked to your parents, a perpetual nonpaying guest whom their son visited every night in her cottage?"

"The Larkins have only respect for you, Jade," he said. Abandoning his playful behavior, he turned her around in his arms and embraced her gently. "Just as I have.

You're the most principled woman I've ever met. It's one of the reasons I love you."

"Is it?" she asked, returning his embrace.

"Of course it is." His kiss was delicious, yet restrained, as though he recognized that he'd offended her. She melted into him, delirious with the feel of his naked skin. When they broke apart finally, she could see in his dark eyes the struggle he waged for control.

"Can you blame me, though," he whispered, "if I can't get enough of that luscious body of yours? You know how difficult it is for me each time I have to leave you?"

Then marry me and you won't have to leave, she wanted to shout. But she didn't. Instead, she appeased him with a few more kisses, then made him breakfast before he departed for the gallery.

Later, when she was selecting her clothes for the day, she glanced in the rear of the closet at the painting which had started this whole new phase of her life. She still didn't know who the woman was, but keeping the painting had become important to her.

As she had several times before, she pulled back the cover and studied the face. The image no longer glared back at her like the portrait of Dorian Gray with its twisted censure for her sins. Instead, she'd begun to feel a sympathetic kinship with the unknown woman. Not as important to her as it seemed to be to Cain, nonetheless, she agreed the painting was somehow connected to her life. When she spoke next to her mother on the phone, she intended to ask about it.

Meantime, she had to resolve her relationship with the man who had just left.

How long could she wait for him to make some permanent commitment? Their lovemaking thrilled her beyond her wildest fantasies and had become even more intimate since, after that first evening, she'd had the good sense to consult a doctor about personal protection. Their passion now stripped of inhibitions, she wasn't worried that the fire in their loins often demanded immediate satiation in places other than a bed.

That next evening was a prime example. Cain dropped by carrying a bottle of wine and a grocery bag containing all the makings for an Italian dinner. Together they sipped wine and worked together preparing what turned out to be a delicious lasagna. The cleanup after dinner evolved into a playful snapping of dish towels which culminated in a round of fiery lovemaking on the kitchen table. Their appetites still unsatisfied, they barely made it to the bedroom before lust consumed their senses once again. Exhausted at last, they fell asleep in each other's arms.

Jade arose early the following morning and was already drying off from her morning shower when Cain finally roused.

"Come here, woman," he growled as she reached to slip into her terry robe.

"Oh, no, Cain," she whined, dodging skillfully out of his grasp, "we don't have time for this. I have a meeting with my new bosses later today and you have a gallery to run." Her resolve weakened by the soulful expression on his face, however, a moment later she was in his arms.

After a lingering kiss, "Now, that'll have to do for now," she said, wriggling to escape.

But the belt of her terry robe snagged between his fingers and by the time she freed herself, her shoulders were almost naked. At once, the belt slid from Cain's grasp and a darkened expression replaced the lust in his features.

"My God, Jade! look at you!" His sharpened outburst startled her so that, instinctively, she grabbed for the robe to cover her nakedness.

"What's wrong?" she solicited in alarm.

"Your back! It looks like I beat you!" With almost harsh fingers, he gripped her shoulders and tore away the plush garment. His sudden action shook the pins from her hair. The freed tresses tumbled down her bare back, but not quickly enough to hide the angry red whelps along her spine and shoulder blades.

"I guess I was too distracted last night to notice," she said, laughing with relief. Still smiling, she reached out and caressed his cheek. "I have a feeling we could find a few scratches on your back, as well."

Seeming to come to himself a little, he released her. But she could tell he was still not placated when he continued in a voice heavy with self-reproach, "Don't ever let me lose myself that way again." To her questioning look, "Making love like some crazed animal," he said, "any decent man would have stopped before he hurt you like that."

"You didn't hurt me," she said. Realizing that arguing with him was not the way to wean him away from this self-deprecation, "But okay, whatever you say, darling." she cooed. In a single rhythmic motion, she pushed her robe completely away and swept the sheet from his naked torso. "I promise, before we get carried away again, I'll let you know if I approve of our playground. She smoothed velvet fingers down his cheek and onto his muscular chest. "How's that?

"Just for the record," she whispered as her fingers began a very creative massage of his sex, "the bed already has my full endorsement."

"Oh, God, Jade, I love you!" With a groan of surrender, he crushed her tightly in his arms. "You beautiful, wondrous creature," he murmured, trailing hungry kisses over her naked body, "I never get enough of you."

More important things than a few superficial wounds consumed their attention during the next several minutes. The first to awaken from their exhausted nap, Jade lay next to Cain studying those finely-chiseled features made softer by sleep. Why had he seemed at once convinced that a few accidental bruises were a result of his darker nature? she wondered. Did he actually fear he might be the product of some flawed genealogy?

Was that the terrible secret that lay behind his foster parents' denial of him? Would such fears prevent him from ever making a permanent commitment to her?

"I'm sorry—about earlier." Almost as if he were aware of her watching him, Cain's eyes opened. "I didn't mean to snap at you. It's just that—"

"I understand," she said. Smiling down at him, she reached out and smoothed a lock of his dark hair. "It's okay, Cain, really, it's okay."

"No, it's not okay." He levered himself up and pushed pillows behind his head. "And you don't understand, not really. But I think you ought to. I think it's time I explain."

"Only if you want to." She propped herself up one elbow and waited.

Sam's brow lifted questioningly. "Are you adopted?"

"No, I'm a foundling, a foster child."

"Well, in that case, the state agency that placed you should have all that—"

"No agencies were involved," Cain noted in interruption, "at least, not any my other sources have been able to find in the U.S. My foster parents have ties outside the States, though. I can give you a list of places in the world where they've done business. That ought to help you determine where else I might have lived when they got me."

Now Sam's look had turned incredulous. "You think somebody mighta just left you with these people?"

"That's what I want you to find out," Cain said.

"Why haven't you asked your foster parents about these things? Or do you have reason to suspect they mighta kidnapped you?"

"That's a possibility, too, I suppose. But, no, my gut feeling tells me they know who my biological parents are and they had permission to take me."

"Your foster parents have any family themselves—brothers, sisters?"

Cain shook his head. "Cy claims he's an orphan and Leona says her parents and her only brother died years ago." He paused, then added, "I have to say, my foster parents seem decent enough. They've done a lot for me, I have to give them that."

Sam raised a skeptical eyebrow. "Sometimes folks you'd think are decent do mighty indecent things. But I'll go on what you say till I find out different." He flipped open his notebook. "Now, what's your full name?"

Assuming that meant the detective would take his case, Cain began, "I don't know exactly what my true name is. I go by Cain Delancy because those are the first two names the Larkins tagged me with. I used their last name until a few years ago when I found out I had no right to it."

The detective's mouth twisted in contemplation. "Do you remember anything about your life before the Larkins took you in?" he asked finally. "Like where you might have lived?"

"No, nothing I can think of. I figure I was about two when they took me in. There are no pictures of me earlier than that that I can find in family albums."

Sam looked Cain up and down. "So all this must have happened about thirty or so years ago?"

Cain nodded. "I'll celebrate my thirty-third birthday soon. And for some reason I believe both my age and my birth date are the true ones."

"Well, if you're willing to go with my people on this, I think we've got a start." He jotted down one last note and closed his book. "What do you say, Mr. Delancy, still want to proceed?"

Cain nodded, then rose from his chair. "That's what I asked you here for. Your rates seem fair and I already know you have a reputation for being discreet. And now that I've talked to you, I'm convinced you're the man who can find out what I want to know."

"We'll see." The beefy detective put away his pen and pad and pushed back his chair. Pausing as he turned to leave, he said, "Mr. Delancy, can I ask you something?"

"Sure."

"You said your foster parents are decent people. They've been good to you, you say." He looked around the spacious office. "And I'd say you're doing all right for yourself these days."

"Everything you say is true," Cain admitted.

The detective's head bobbed up and down. "Have you ever thought it might be better to leave well enough alone?"

"Yes, I have," Cain had to own, as well. "And I've tried living without knowing.

But I just can't do it anymore. Well enough just isn't good enough. I have to know."

Sam Flaherty eyed him a second more. "Even though it may cost me a job," he said finally, "I gotta be frank with you, Mr. Delancy. In a lot of cases with foster children, the birth parents are the kind of people you wouldn't want to know about. The couple who raised you may have been doing you a favor by covering things up."

Cain nodded. "That's the very thing I'm afraid of."

Bushy eyebrows lifted again. "Then, why are you pressing to find out what your foster family obviously doesn't want you to know?"

Cain sucked in a long breath. "Because I want a life and I know I'll never have it if I don't find out the truth."

The other man heaved a prodigious sigh. "Okay. It's your money. But I'd be willing to bet you'll be sorry."

"Cain let out his own breath in a resounding echo. "No bet, Sam, no bet."

CHAPTER EIGHT

"Are you saying you and Cain aren't getting married?"

Leona Larkin's voice faltered as if she were on the verge of weeping. Jade felt even more guilty about her errand with Cain parents now that she realized how grossly they'd misinterpreted her purpose.

Only moments after the maitre-d had seated them at a table in this charming little restaurant, Leona had begun prompting her to reveal plans for a wedding. She'd managed to sidestep their hints during the meal, but finally she'd decided there was no alternative except to be blunt.

"I'm sorry you got the wrong impression," she offered in apology. "I didn't dream you would assume things had gone as far as marriage with your son. But the truth is, Cain hasn't proposed marriage, and I'm not sure I would accept if he did."

"Oh, my dear, whatever makes you say that?" Leona sounded even more tortured.

She cast a glance at her husband, who, like her, resembled a naughty puppy who'd just been whacked with a rolled-up newspaper.

"I don't understand," Cy spoke up when his wife seemed unable to continue, "you and Cain seem very much in love with each other."

"Cain tells me he loves me," Jade admitted. "And I think he does—as much as he's able."

Leona whisked another worried glance in her husband's direction and cleared her throat. "Oh my, I've always worried about Cain's reluctance to show his feelings. Even as a child he seemed unwilling to give too much of himself. I'd hoped he wouldn't be so stingy with you."

"Doesn't he have good reason to hold back his feelings?" Jade asked with a little more harshness than she'd intended.

"Why, Jade, what makes you say a thing like that?" Leona's eyes widened in what seemed genuine shock.

Jade's tender heart forced her to pull some of the teeth from her attack. "I'm sorry, I didn't mean to imply that you don't love your son. And I realize I have no right to pry into your relationship with him. But I love him, too. And I want more than anything for us to have a future together. The problem is, I doubt if he can ever make a commitment to me as long as he feels rejected by his family."

"We've never meant for Cain to feel rejected." Cy filled in the void while Leona continued to fight off tears. "We've tried to treat him as our own in every way."

"Not in every way, it seems," Jade challenged. "You've never adopted him, never legally given him your name."

When Leona raised her head, Jade saw that her face was pale, her features etched with pain. Cy's features showed distress, as well, mixed with concern for his wife. For a moment, the older couple looked at one another, their eyes locked in silent communication. Then Cy took both his wife's hands in his and said quietly, "It's okay, honey, we can tell her."

Still clutching her husband's hand, Leona turned to face Jade.

"My dear girl," she started in a shaky spurt, "we were so pleased when you and Cain became close. He's never shown any serious interest in a woman before. We," she glanced at Cy, "we know you've made him happier these past weeks than he's ever been. We've already begun to think of you as a member of our family."

"You've been wonderful to me," Jade affirmed, touched that they returned her warm feelings. "You've treated me with as much kindness as my own family. But I don't understand—"

"Because we've come to think so well of you," Leona continued before Jade could finish, "we believe we can count on you not to repeat anything we tell you."

"Of course you can," she assured. "You have my word."

Leona sighed with relief, then proceeded to explain, "We want you to know we love Cain, every bit as much as our natural son, Daniel. But as I said earlier, Cain has always had trouble expressing his feelings for us. We assumed we'd created part of the problem early on by telling him he was adopted."

When Jade eyed the other woman questioningly, "Oh, yes," she said, "for most of his life we kept up the pretense that we'd legally adopted Cain. He only ceased using our last name a few years ago. He ran into some difficulties getting a passport, and he asked to see his adoption papers."

The older woman expelled another heavy sigh. "Naturally, we had to admit that there were no adoption papers. We tried to assure Cain that we'd only kept up the deception for his own good. We loved him and a few legal documents didn't change that. But nothing we said seemed to convince him. It was as if he'd always suspected something was wrong and now this proved it."

"I still don't understand," Jade said, puzzled, "are you saying there really is something wrong with him, that it's the reason you've never given him your name?"

"Oh, my goodness, no." Leona shook her head vigorously. "It has nothing to do with Cain. We didn't adopt him because," she bolstered her courage with another glance at Cy, who nodded his support for her to continue, "because at the time he came to us, the circumstances were—well, it just wasn't possible."

"What circumstances?" Jade felt more enmeshed by the minute in a web of confusion. "And what about later on, didn't there come a time when you could have proceeded with an adoption?"

Leona held tightly to her husband's hand, seeming to need his strength to say what she had to. "We never adopted Cain because we couldn't," she said. "He was never given up for adoption."

Suddenly aware that she'd leaned steadily forward as Leona spoke, Jade sat back heavily in her chair. She stared at the couple across from her in shocked disbelief. "You can't mean you stole Cain from his natural parents?" she had to know.

Again Leona hastened her denial. "Of course we didn't. We were given legal custody along with power of attorney by his natural father. The boy's mother had given up all parental rights when she left, which was years before the boy was turned over to us.

"You see, Cain's father is my stepbrother," she clarified. "When circumstances made it impossible for him to take care of his son any longer, he signed over most of what he owned to us and asked us to raise his child. We were more than willing to adopt the boy, but my stepbrother didn't want that. He made me promise I would never pursue the matter."

"Is Cain's father still alive?" Jade asked.

"Yes, he is," Leona answered.

"And is he the artist who painted my face and those other pictures Cain found?"

The older woman nodded.

"Why can't you just tell Cain about all this now, at least let him know what became of his father? The man's not in prison or anything, is he?"

"Oh, no, he never went to prison."

"Then, why not tell Cain what happened to separate him from his parents? You must realize it's destroying him not to know."

Leona looked helpless. "I can't, Jade. It was part of my promise to my stepbrother not to tell his son about him. I can't even tell Cain his father is alive."

Leona's look had become anxious. "And you mustn't tell him, either, my dear."

"I gave you my word," Jade was quick to assure, "and I'll keep it. I won't tell him anything about our conversation today."

The older woman nodded. "You must see, we hate that it must be this way, but if anything is revealed, the estate that rightfully belongs to Cain becomes forfeit—the gallery, the land, everything. And even if I could share some of the story with him, I don't know where his father is. My stepbrother didn't want us to know his whereabouts after he left us, and we've never tried to find out. All we know is he gets in touch with the attorney from time to time. Other than that, he might as well have vanished off the face of the earth. She sighed resignedly. "And considering the problems he had at the time, I suppose it was the only thing he could do."

"Do you think he ever intended to make things up with Cain?"

"All I know is, he said he would—when the time was right."

"Surely, Jade, you can understand our position," Cy offered, "the power to change things with Cain is not in our hands. We would do anything for our sons, give over everything we have if it would make things right. But we're bound by the trust we entered into when we took Cain as our own. Betraying it now would not only deny him his birthright, but destroy what we might be able to give him, as well."

"How can that be possible?" Jade asked.

"The majority of our personal holdings," Leona explained, "is bound up in money we invested from my stepbrother's estate. He knew our import business needed serious money to move forward quickly, and he wanted us to have the means to raise his son properly. He gave us those funds when he left. The only stipulation to our acceptance of the money was that we had to keep his secrets. If we had to give up that cash to pay back the estate, our business would be devastated."

"It's not that we're greedy," Cy added, "but Leona and I have spent over half our lives building up a business so we'd have something to pass along to both our sons. We can't just let all of that go." His face took on the same helpless look as his wife's. "It all comes back to the same problem. We can't alter the situation without making more problems. And whatever we might concede to do can only harm Cain more, that's all we can say."

Jade didn't quite understand even yet. There was something neither of the Larkins was willing to tell—the underlying secret which had forced this whole arrangement that Leona had alluded to. But they'd already entrusted her with a great part of this dreadful dilemma. How could she press them to tell any more?

"Then, I'm now bound just like you to keep silent?" she ventured.

The couple nodded in unison. Leona forced a sad smile. "I'm sorry, Jade. We know how cruel this must seem. But if you reveal what we've said here today, it would be the same as our betraying it ourselves. So we must ask you to keep our trust."

Almost to herself, Jade murmured, "I'd hoped I might find a way to reassure Cain." When she lifted her head and saw the uneasy looks on the Larkins' faces, she spoke up hastily, "Don't worry, I won't tell him anything I've learned today."

"Jade, dear," Leona said after a minute, "I'd think just knowing you love him would be enough to make Cain forget all this worry about his past."

"I haven't told him I love him," Jade confessed.

Leona looked worried again. "But why not, my dear. If you really do love him, as you've said, shouldn't you tell him?"

Jade shrugged. "I believe commitment goes with a declaration of love."

"And you can't commit to Cain?" his foster mother asked anxiously. "Is that it?"

Jade thought for a moment before she answered. Had anything she'd learned made a difference in the way she felt about Cain? If he asked her now, could she commit to marriage, even accept his reservations about himself in the bargain?

"I didn't feel certain I could before," she said at last, "but now, yes, I'm sure I can commit to a life with Cain. I love him, that's all that matters, and I'm going to tell him so."

A pair of enormous smiles replaced the concerned frowns on the faces of Cain's foster parents. "We knew you two loved each other." Leona, as usual, voiced both their feelings. "We could tell by the way you look at one another. And you're the right girl for Cain, we're even more sure of that than before."

For the next several minutes, Jade allowed the two older people to shower her with their good wishes. They'd tried to do the right thing by their son. She no longer doubted their love for Cain or their desire for his happiness. And she'd gained a fresh optimism that he would eventually see that, as well. Surrounded by the light of her love, one day he'd let go of the darkness forever.

Perhaps, though, she should call her mother, anyway. Just to satisfy herself that her parent knew nothing about this situation that might come out later and harm Cain. If nothing else, it would reassure her that she'd done all she could to erase the shadows in Cain's life.

"Maybe our son had the right idea," Leona suggested, "maybe it is more than a coincidence that you resemble a girl in a portrait his father painted."

Alerted, Jade stared at the older woman. How had she forgotten that? It could be another key to this whole matter. "About that, I meant to ask you—" She cut short her own statement when she glimpsed from across the room the maitre-d pointing in their direction. Even as her gaze attached to the man he was speaking to, she'd already guessed it was Cain. She barely had time to turn back to her two companions and whisper, "Your son is here," before she saw him nod at the waiter and start toward their table.

Handsome in a dark wool suit and maroon tie, he might have been a cover model for the successful business executive. However, the grim look which had seized control of his features thwarted the perfection of his grooming. Trying to assign some name to his stony expression, she realized it was as if his face had been dipped in plaster and emerged a hardened mask.

Perhaps Cain's foster parents failed to notice; perhaps they'd grown so accustomed to his moodiness they no longer paid any attention. Whatever the reason, Cy and Leona reacted with a friendly greeting, as though they viewed his sudden appearance as a welcome intrusion.

He returned their salutations with the emotionless courtesy Jade had hoped not to see again. Even that taut response was better than the curt acknowledgement he flung in her direction. The stone coldness in his eyes reminded her of the chill that look had evoked at their first meeting.

"You've got yourself a fine young woman here, son," Cy spoke up in a tone of oblivious good humor. "We've just been having a nice little chat with her."

"Oh, is that so?" Cain retorted, his solid tone debased by its sarcastic echo. "And now I suppose everybody knows everything about everybody else?" As he spoke, his gaze glided over Jade like a finely honed blade which cuts with such precision the victim scarcely believes the blood oozing from his wound.

"I called your office to ask if you might get away for lunch," he told her, an undercurrent of accusation in his tone. "Your secretary was very helpful. She told me I'd find you here. She seemed surprised, though, that I hadn't been invited to come along."

"It turns out business meetings pretty much emptied my classes this afternoon." Jade said, trying to make this gathering sound spur-of-the moment. "So I thought I'd take a chance that Cy and Leona might be free for lunch. Ignoring his sour countenance, she smiled prettily. "I thought it was about time I paid your folks back for all those wonderful meals I've enjoyed at their house."

"How nice," he said with shallow courtesy. "Well then, since you have the rest of the afternoon free, you have time to go for drive with me, don't you?" His invitation sounded very much like a dare.

"But you haven't had any lunch," she pointed out in a desperate attempt to delay the confrontation she knew was about to erupt. "And we just can't hurry off and leave your parents."

For moments, he seemed to wrestle with the demands of good manners. At the same time, Jade searched vainly for a means to smooth this situation. Cain already suspected an ulterior motive in her actions since she hadn't informed him about her lunch date. She felt another nudge of guilt because he'd caught her this way. She'd promised his parents she wouldn't reveal the nature of their conversation. What could she say when Cain asked, as he inevitably would, what had been going on? Prostituting her integrity contradicted her nature so completely she doubted she had the skill to make up an outright lie. If she merely flirted with the truth, would he accept what she told him without more questions? Not likely, she surmised, still struggling to meet his cold stare.

"I'm sure the Larkins will excuse us," he clipped, effectively severing the slim rope of safety this public place provided. "And I don't think I want any lunch. Suddenly, I'm not at all hungry." He gripped the back of her chair. "Cy, Leona," he said with the barest civility, "you don't mind if Jade and I visit awhile on our own, do you?"

"Of course we don't mind," Leona said, nodding encouragement to both younger people. Like her husband, she seemed utterly blind to Cain's threatening demeanor. "You two lovebirds don't worry about us. Just run along and have a nice afternoon."

Cain's steel fingers around Jade's arm as he ushered her from the restaurant didn't make her feel like she was loved. She felt more like some mobster's hostage being hustled off on one of those rides that usually ends with only one of them coming back.

Nevertheless, she didn't struggle to wrench her arm free. She and Cain had to start understanding one another if this relationship were to continue. His heavy silence inside the Jeep renewed her uneasy feeling of a doomsday ride. And she could tell by the countryside whizzing past the windows that they weren't headed toward her apartment. Instead, this road led to his property. She wanted to ask why he preferred such a remote spot to talk, but she didn't. The chances of a civil reply at this moment were about as great as these mountains suddenly wearing to dust.

Even after he brought the Jeep to a halt beside the grove of pines he'd arranged to sell, Cain didn't speak. He heaved a long sigh, then sat for interminable minutes with the steering wheel clutched in a white-knuckled grip. Finally, like a robot whose timing device had clicked on, he flung open the driver's side door. And before Jade hardly realized what was happening, he hopped out of the vehicle and reappeared seconds later on the passenger side.

"Let's walk," he said in the old "that's an order" tone of weeks ago, then yanked open her door. He barely spared her a cursory glance before he grabbed her hand in a hold that again smacked more of control than affection.

"No," she heard her own voice answer, at the same time jerking her hand away.

"What?" At least her unexpected rebuff induced him to look at her.

"Whatever you have to say, you may as well say it right here," she told him flatly. She wasn't afraid now, but she was getting angry. "I don't know what you think you're doing, but I'm not tramping through the woods in this outfit."

As if he'd only now thought about it, Cain snapped his thunderous gaze to her snug-fitting skirt and high-heel pumps. His eyebrows pinched in pained annoyance, and, for seconds, he seemed to think over this dilemma. Finally, with a sigh of exasperation, he reached in and scooped her into his arms and struck out across the wilderness.

He was hardly dressed for a trek in the woods himself, Jade noticed when her surprise subsided (she'd briefly considered demanding he put her down, but in his present frame of mind, he might just take her literally). Seeming not to mind that the cuffs of his slacks were being soiled by the untamed underbrush, he marched with amazing agility over the rough ground. Though even her slight weight had to be cumbersome, his steps never slowed even through the matted thickets. He uttered not one further word, even after they reached the clearing where they'd shared such a wonderful picnic only weeks before.

In contrast to his frame of mind, his arms were gentle when he set her down on a rock that nature had hewn into a crude throne. Still without a word, he turned away and began to pace in front of her like a vassal before a queen, who can't bring himself to ask if she meant to take away everything that was important to him.

Jade sat quietly and waited for Cain to work through some of his emotions. She looked around. The area had changed only slightly since the day they'd picnicked here. Half the month of October had passed, yet the hardwoods barely showed the first blush of autumn color. The breeze playing among the pines felt cool and soothing. Only the grim silence of her companion disturbed the gentle comfort of this place.

"They want you to break things off with me, don't they?" he blurted out at last.

"What?" Jade thought she'd prepared herself for anything he might accuse her of, but the conclusion he'd jumped to startled her.

"They did no such thing," she protested in immediate response. "Whatever gave you the idea your parents might suggest we end our relationship?"

He shrugged. "You're a nice girl from a conservative background. That makes you vulnerable. They have to have recognized that by now. And they must know things have gotten pretty serious between us, so it's natural they'd try to warn you off before your closeness to me caused you harm."

Cain's harsh assessment of himself so confounded her, several minutes passed before she was able to collect her thoughts. She was about to reply when he cut her off with another raw-edged assault.

"Why did you sneak around behind my back to meet them, anyway? Were you already having doubts about me even before you listened to what the Larkins had to say?"

That accusation sparked anger, but Jade tamped down the blaze before it flared.

"Meeting for lunch at a popular restaurant, which, also, happens to be a favorite of your parents, hardly constitutes sneaking around," she said, amazing herself at the measure of calm in her voice. "I didn't tell you I planned to meet them because I had a feeling you might read something clandestine into it. I see I was right."

He passed on a counter to that point; instead, he launched a fresh assault. "Why did you do it, Jade? Did you just have to know if there was something tainted about me?"

She had to bite hard into her lower lip to hold back a sharp retort that time. "It's nothing like that," she managed, still with reasonable calm. "I met with Cy and Leona because I felt I had to appeal to them personally to tell me why they couldn't adopt you, that's all. I thought it might help if I could get them to share more information about their reasons."

He looked less than convinced by that explanation. "Really?" he asked warily. "And did they give you more than the flimsy account they've tried to make me believe all these years?"

Her senses winced from the pinch of that question. Her only hope, she realized, was to persuade him to turn loose of the subject before her promise to his parents forced her into an outright lie.

"I don't know what story you're talking about," she hedged. "The way Cy and Leona explained things to me, they had no choice in the matter. Some legal problem with your biological family, as I understand it, made adoption out of the question. They claim they acted in the only way they could, and I believe them. They realize you blame them for never trying to change things, and that bothers them a lot.

"It bothers me, too, Cain," she said in a desperate attempt to entice him away from this dangerous topic. "That's the main reason I decided to talk to them alone."

Throwing off her peace offering, he shot back, "Don't you think I have a right to resent this limbo existence I'm trapped inside? Can't you see it's important to me to know what my name is?"

"Of course you have reason to feel resentful. And I do understand your need to find out who you are. But I don't agree that you should let it rule your life. Whatever their mistakes, the Larkins love you, I'm more convinced than ever that that's true. It's the most important thing I learned from them. They're your family now, and that's all that should matter."

He ceased his incessant pacing and came to stand in front of her. "But don't you see, Jade," he said almost in a plea, "they're not my family, not like people understand family to be? Everybody, no matter how great their relationship, can assign his existence to two people." He rubbed the back of his neck impatiently. "I don't even know if Cain Delancy is any part of my real name. Cy and Leona won't give me the answers I need. But I'm going to find out those answers—all of them."

Jade shot up from her seat, as though a lightning bolt had creased the solid rock beneath her. "Cain, what do you mean, you're going to find out? What are you planning to do?"

"I've already started doing it. I've hired a private investigator to find out anything he can about where I came from."

"Oh, no, Cain! You haven't! You mustn't do that!" The impact of her emotions sabotaging any attempt at control now, the words tore from her lips in an anguished appeal. "You have to call off this investigation. Leave this whole thing alone. Please."

Clearly astonished by this outburst, Cain stared at her. "Why must I leave it alone? I have to know who I am, haven't I been able to make you understand that? I should have pursued this more forcefully a long time ago." His head cocked at a curious angle, and she saw suspicion re-enter his countenance. "Or have you kept something back that Cy and Leona told you," he asked, "something you don't want me to find out?"

"No, no, it's not that." Jade realized she teetered dangerously close to that lie she'd been trying to avoid. Nevertheless, she had to reassure Cain. "It's just that I'm afraid they'll be hurt if you go poking into things that should probably be left alone.

"Besides," she offered in a lighter tone, "there can't be anything about your family that makes you less of a man than you've made of yourself, so why worry about it? Cy and Leona love you for the person you are." She reached out and touched his cheek. "And I love you, too, Cain."

Instantly alert, his stormy eyes sped headlong into the jade depths of hers.

"I do love you, Cain," she said again. "I'd already admitted it to myself even before we made love that first time."

For what seemed an eternity, his gaze probed the green mist. Then his breath released in a heavy sigh, and he reached out and hauled her into his arms.

"Oh, Jade, Jade, darling," he whispered, stroking the silken strands of her hair, "I thought you were too afraid of me to risk loving me."

"I'm not afraid of you, Cain." She pulled slightly away from his embrace so he couldn't miss the sincerity behind her words. "It's just that, for me, love means a commitment, the most important commitment I ever plan to make, the one I hope will last a lifetime. I was wrong that other time when I thought a man returned my feelings;

all he wanted was to use me to get something he wanted. I couldn't risk that happening again. I had to be sure what you wanted was me before I said anything."

Returning her gaze with unflinching steadiness, he said, "Oh, honey, I knew almost from the first I was never going to be able to let you go. It is you I want, Jade, for always."

Thank God, Jade offered up in silent gratitude. She hadn't misplaced her heart this time. Cain had responded in the way she'd hoped with a true commitment. Now they could start building that future she'd always wanted.

"I'm yours, my darling," she said, surrendering gladly into his arms. "Forever."

When his lips sealed possession of the gift she had bestowed, no queen could have asked for a more steadfast pledge from her knight than the one his kiss promised.

"I love you, don't ever forget that," he murmured, than commended his body to proving it again.

Sunlight sparkled in her hair as Cain drowned his fingers in the rivulets of shimmering tresses. Her body, pliant and eager to receive his passion, swayed against him, reveling in his instant response. She felt through his trousers a more urgent demand in the swelling hardness of his loins.

When he broke away, he was barely able to gasp, "We have to get home."

Nodding, she whispered, "Yes, and quickly."

No doubts existed in Jade's mind that she and Cain would make love when they reached the privacy of her apartment, a more binding lovemaking than they'd ever enjoyed. Like a teenager asserting possession of his steady, Cain kept one arm tightly around her while with the other he guided the Jeep back toward town. Both of them were literally shaking with anticipation when they finally reached her bedroom. The instant their senses began to explode in another magical extravaganza, Jade was convinced she'd been right. This wasn't a mere physical joining; this was two people expressing love, not just for the satiation of the flesh, but for the fulfillment of their hearts, as well.

Their most clamorous appetites appeased for the time being, they rested for minutes in each others arms. Glowing with the experience of true love, Jade suddenly realized she'd neglected her man in another way.

"You must be starving," she said aloud.

Cain turned toward her, chuckling. "I was, but I'm feeling mighty satisfied right now."

She pushed up on one elbow and smiled down at him. "I'm not talking about that, not for the time being, anyway. I mean food. You didn't have any lunch and now it's past dinnertime. Why don't you rest while I go fix us something?"

"Oh, no, I'm not letting you get away from me that easily," he said, hugging her to him and rocking her in his arms.

"I'm hungry for a little food, too, after all this," she said, giggling. "Besides, I may need your services again before the evening is over and I don't want you to give out on me."

He laughed and kissed her hair. "Good point. Let's go see what's in your refrigerator."

Wearing barely enough clothes to appease modesty, they worked together to prepare a simple meal of cold cuts, fruit and cheeses. Cain lighted a fire in the hearth and put some soft music on the stereo while Jade spread their repast on the living room floor.

Feeding each other from the platter of tasty tidbits started a pleasurable teasing, but it wasn't long before the teasing awakened more erotic cravings, and the needs of their stomachs lost out to a different epicurean delight. Much later, still bound in each other's arms, they collapsed into exhausted sleep.

For the next two days, the lovers hardly left one another's company. Jealous of any intrusion from the outside, they cooked or ordered in when they felt the need for additional fortification.

Late Sunday evening, Jade reluctantly allowed Cain to part from her. She took some comfort in the anticipation of a time soon when she would never again have to let him go.

Apparent that his thoughts had traveled along the same path, he pulled her to him and murmured, "Oh, Jade, I wish we could get married tomorrow."

Straining from his arms, she stared at him. “It won’t be long, will it?”

He looked at her with saddened eyes. “I hope not, sweetheart.”

The strangeness of his reply even more confusing, she searched his eyes. “You hope not?” she asked. “What do you mean by that? This state doesn’t have a long waiting period for marriage licenses, does it?”

She felt his body stiffen and saw his features tense. “Jade, I thought you understood,” he said in pained reply, “we have to wait, at least until this private detective gives me some news. How can I offer you my name when I don’t even know if I have one fit to give? No, darling, I can’t ask you to marry me, not until I know who I am.”

CHAPTER NINE

"What did you say his name was?" Despite the thousands of miles that separated them, Jade couldn't mistake the catch in her mother's voice.

"His name is Cain Delancy," she repeated. "Why, *Mama*? Have you heard the name before? His family owns an import business and an art gallery here in Atlanta."

Jade had written to her mother and explained some of the recent changes in her life. However, aside from mentioning that she'd become interested in a man she'd met here in Atlanta, she hadn't spoken about Cain by name until now. Her mother was not very fond of long distance phone calls; they seemed to upset her somehow. Jade had hoped to be able to relay the good news of a wedding date to reassure her parent when she made this call.

However, considering recent events, a time when that might take place was far from certain. She needed to hear her mother's voice, to seek some kind of advice from the only loving parent she had left. If Kellus Hartman could shed any light on this mystery surrounding Cain's life, she had to know about it right away.

Several seconds of dead air had elapsed since Jade's last question. "No, no, I'm not acquainted with any family named Delancy," her mother said finally in what seemed a measured response. "I did know of a family from New Orleans by that name long ago, but..." She let the remark trail off without finishing. After another pause she spoke up again, "How did you happen to meet this man, Jade? Is he about your age?"

"A few years older, he's nearly thirty-three," Jade said. "And you're not going to believe this, *Mama*, but I met him because of a painting—a painting that looks like me."

Briefly, she recounted the incident of her first encounter with Cain. "At first, he thought you might have posed for the portrait," she explained, "but when I showed him your photograph, he could see that you and I don't look much alike."

The telephone line went silent for seconds more. Finally, after clearing her throat, Kellus Hartman spoke up again. "No, darling, we don't look much alike, do we? It's just an odd coincidence, I suppose, your looking like some woman in a painting."

"And you don't have any idea who the woman in the painting might be?" Jade prompted. "She really could be my twin. I don't resemble any long lost relative you've never told me about, do I?" she added teasingly.

"No, darling, I have no one, except for you." There was no hint of amusement in Kellus Hartman's reply. After another pause, she asked, "Is it really serious between you and this young man?"

"Yes, *Mama*, I'm very serious about him. In fact, I'm in love with him."

"And you're thinking about marrying him?" Her mother's tone sounded anxious now.

"I'd like to marry him, yes. We love each other. But there's a problem, one that may force us to postpone any plans for marriage. It's very complicated and I don't know how to explain it except to tell you it's an issue with his family. The painting I mentioned may be a part of a mystery concerning his family's history, but I don't know how. That's why I've been putting all these questions to you.

"Maybe you've heard of Cy and Leona Larkin?" Jade paused a second, hoping her mother might respond to that name, but she heard nothing other than a slight intake of breath at the other end. "Cain was brought up by the Larkins, you see," she went on, "but he's determined to know who his biological parents are. It's so important to him he won't consider starting a life with me until he finds out. I'd almost say he's obsessed about it."

"And has he found out anything yet?" her mother asked.

"No. The Larkins won't discuss it with him. I think Cain's afraid their reticence might mean there's something criminal involved with his family. It doesn't matter to me who his birth family is," she added when she could no longer hide her anguish. "He's the man I've chosen to spend my life with. What happened thirty years ago shouldn't affect our lives, should it, *Mama*?"

"No, *ma petite*, what might have happened a long time ago shouldn't matter now." Jade heard emotion in her mother's voice, as well. "You just keep telling your young man that."

"I will, *Mama*," Jade said. "I only hope that someday he'll believe me."

Their conversation hadn't put to rest Jade's uncertainties, as she'd hoped it would. Kellus Hartman had denied any knowledge of Cain's family, and her mother had never lied to her in the past. Yet something Jade had noted in her parent's reactions made her uneasy. Maybe her mother *did* know who the subject of the portrait was. Maybe it was a relative who had shamed her family in some way. Kellus Hartman had always claimed to be the only surviving member of an old New Orleans family, but thirty years ago might she have had a sister who had been disowned and, therefore, was never acknowledged?

"Goodbye, *Mama,* I'll be with you for Christmas, I promise," she said, replacing the telephone receiver thoughtfully.

Should she now press the Larkins for added information? Jade wondered. Perhaps the couple could be persuaded to tell her more. Perhaps if she brought up her mother directly, they might react. Only slightly bolstered by this latest resolve, she heaved a long sigh. She had to do something. This waiting made her feel as much in limbo as Cain felt. Her high hopes that the two of them might have permanence in their future were fading more and more as each day passed without their being any closer to the truth.

Another thought did cheer her. Cain's thirty-third birthday was approaching. Perhaps a party in his honor with some of his closest friends might be good for both of them. With renewed resolve, she lifted the receiver again and dialed Leona Larkin's office.

"What do you think?" she asked after she'd presented her party suggestion to Cain's foster mother. "Do you think he'd respond well to my idea?"

"I think it's a wonderful suggestion," Leona agreed. "Especially since it comes from you."

"Doesn't Cain like birthday parties?" Jade asked.

"Oh, he enjoys getting together with his friends," Leona explained, "but he hasn't seemed to appreciate our making a fuss about his birthday, not in recent years. I'm sure you can guess why."

"Yes, I can," Jade murmured. She paused, thinking again how awkward her position had become. So many secrets she couldn't reveal. She'd sworn not to tell Cain what the Larkins had shared with her. And now Cain had exacted her promise not to let on that he'd hired a private investigator. The burdens were growing heavy on her shoulders and she couldn't seem to rid herself of any of them.

"Well, maybe we should start changing some things," she announced to Leona with forced optimism. "I, for one, am ready to get on with the future. Now, about this party, can I count on you to take care of the invitations? You know Cain's friends better than I do. We can work together on the rest of the details. How'll that be? Will you give me a hand?"

"You bet I will," Leona agreed, her optimism sounding genuine. "I'm really excited now about the whole idea. It's very good of you to do this, my dear."

Jade felt more guilt heaped on her when she hung up the phone. Leona had thanked her over and over for her caring gesture. She didn't feel like a caring person. After the disaster she'd left behind in Washington, she'd hoped never again to have to deal with hurtful secrets. Now circumstances had trapped her in a web of secrets that could possibly hurt everyone she loved.

By the time Cain's birthday arrived, Jade felt better. Everyone on the guest list had agreed to join the celebration. Persuading the guest of honor to go with her to his parents' house for dinner that evening turned out to be her biggest problem.

"I want to spend my birthday with you," he insisted. "Cy and Leona know I don't expect any kind of celebration so they won't miss us."

"But your parents have told me they have a special present for you," she finally had to divulge, though she'd promised to remain mum about that, as well. "Leona has prepared your favorite meal and arranged for a cake. I'd feel terrible if we didn't at least put in an appearance after she's gone to so much trouble. We'll leave early if you want." she added to head off any more objections.

"All right," he agreed with obvious reluctance. "If it means that much to you, I suppose we can stop by for awhile."

"What's wrong with me?" Cain demanded, verbalizing his frustration as he pulled the Lincoln into the driveway in front of Jade's apartment. Lately, he'd found it more and more difficult to snap out of his dark moods. Jade had merely asked him to attend a birthday dinner. How many dozens of those had he managed to survive? Why couldn't he just have agreed to this one without making her feel as if she'd coerced him?

His fears were suffocating the love of this beautiful, magical woman. Jade gave herself to him as freely as ever. But the joy had disappeared from their lovemaking. Joy had disappeared from every part of their relationship because of him. His darkness had squeezed out its substance.

Standing in front of her door ready to knock, he felt terror slice through him like sharp-edged blade. What if Jade tired of waiting? The best detective in the state might not find out anything about his father. How long could a perfect creature like her remain tethered to an imperfect being like him before her need for happiness tore her away?

"Get it together, man," he counseled. "Try to be cheerful tonight even if you can't feel it." Inhaling a deep breath, he raised his hand and knocked.

"Let's not go inside."

The words flying in the face of the spoken promise Cain had made to Jade earlier, he was balking again at his parents' front door like a prisoner about to be guillotined.

His mood when he appeared at her apartment had stoked her optimism that the evening would go well. He'd been charming and sensually playful to the point that she'd almost canceled their date at the Larkins herself. While appreciating the clinging wisp of coral chiffon she'd chosen for tonight's affair, his eyes had licked over the lines of her body as if he'd more enjoy tearing it off that very second. It had required every ounce of her resolve to put him off.

But delaying their time together would make things even better between them. They would have a wonderful time at his party, then Cain's good humor would restore the old joy to their lovemaking. That had kept her focused. Now her plans seemed about to topple like birthday presents stacked on a rickety table.

"We won't stay any longer than you want, I promise," she said, trying again to appease her date. "I have a little birthday present of my own in mind," she added with a seductive flutter of her eyelashes, "I made you a cake, too, and I have a lot of leftover icing." She curled her fingers around his neck and whispered next to his ear, "But you won't get to see what I have in mind for it if you give me any more trouble."

"Oh, all right." He chuckled lightly, however, the slight shiver she felt through his clothing told her she'd gotten to him. "But I don't promise to behave myself for long."

"Neither do I," she volleyed back with a wink. "Happy birthday, darling," she whispered as they walked through the double front doors together. "And many happy returns!"

The sounds of voices raised in laughter and raucous conversation drowned out his response. Suddenly, someone in the crowd shouted Cain's name and a round of applause burst out. At the same time, what resembled a small ticker tape celebration erupted in the main hall. Colored balloons and confetti rained down. Male and female voices mixed in a crazy round of "Happy Birthday" as Cain's friends descended on him. His smile now definitely genuine, he accepted kisses and handshakes from a bevy of well-wishers.

Jade caught her companion's eye long enough to mouth the words, "I love you." before the crowd sucked him into the festivities.

"This party seems to be just what you needed, my love," she mused a short time later when she saw Cain laugh out loud at one's of his friend's stories. She'd been introduced earlier to most of the group. They'd all responded with polite friendliness, but several odd glances had been cast in Cain's direction.

Their behavior disturbed her. How many of these people had seen the portrait of her double while it still hung in the gallery? Had Cain explained the coincidence to any of them? Or had he simply let them draw their own conclusions?

"May I have your attention?" Leona's attempt to make herself heard over the confusion enticed Jade away from her thoughts. Although Cain's foster mother had shared equally in the preparations for this celebration, she and Cy had remained in the background until now. "May I have your attention, please?" This time her efforts prompted a relay of "sh-h-hs" throughout the crowd.

"Cy and I have a special gift for you, Cain," Leona went on when she had everyone's attention. "Happy birthday, son."

Her words must have cued the man who now emerged from a side door. He was shorter than Cain and stockier in build. Although the dinner jacket he wore was an excellent fit, he looked like the kind of guy who preferred more casual attire. In sharp contrast to Cain's dark features, his were light, his hair so pale that only the glint from the chandelier affirmed the presence of eyebrows.

"Happy birthday, little brother," boomed from his smiling lips. Until this second, Jade hadn't guessed the Larkins' surprise present was his older brother, Daniel.

The two men crossed the room toward each other, but it was Daniel who reached out first. Perhaps no one except Jade noticed the pinch in Cain's brow a second before he succumbed to his brother's embrace.

"Good to see you, man," Cain said, his cordial greeting obviously sincere. "It's been a long time since you paid us a visit. I hear you've added a lot of cash to the Larkin fortune, though."

"Our interests in Canada and overseas do keep me pretty busy." If Daniel took offense at his brother's bluntness, his tone didn't show it. "From what I hear, I'm not the only son in this family who's doing well. Dad tells me your gallery is such a success you're thinking about expanding. You always did have a sixth sense about spotting good pieces of art." He reached out his hand and slapped Cain affectionately on the back. "I'm proud of you, little brother."

By this time, several people in the crowd who seemed to know Daniel had pushed forward to offer their greetings. Jade watched while kisses and handshakes and a few introductions put Cain's brother in touch with the guests.

"Now, I want you to meet someone very special," Cain said. He directed his sibling's attention to where Jade stood slightly apart from the others. "This is Jade Hartman," he announced, curling a possessive arm around her shoulders. "Jade, my brother, Daniel Larkin."

Although he hadn't said, "foster brother," again Cain had emphasized the different last names, Jade noticed. Did he feel like an outsider to Daniel, as well?

"*Ah, la belle dame aux yeux, verte et mysterius*, the beautiful lady with the mysterious green eyes," Daniel offered charmingly. When she extended her hand, he brought the proffered appendage lightly to his lips. "*Enchante, mademoiselle*."

"*Enchante, monsieur, and merci pour la flatterie*," she returned in appreciation of his compliment.

"*Ah, vous parlez francais*?" he said with obvious delight that she spoke French.

"*Oui, monsieur, je parle francais tres bien,* " she said, assuring him she understood. France was home to me for much of my life."

He laughed good-humoredly. "And here I thought I was being suave with my meager knowledge of French."

She laughed, too. "You speak it well enough to make me nostalgic."

"My friends in Quebec think I'm pitiful," he said. "But I'm trying to learn. Perhaps you won't mind letting me practice with you while I'm here."

She offered him a slight bow. "It would be my pleasure, Daniel."

"Jade's a very skilled interpreter," Cain cut in. She felt his grip on her shoulders tighten. "From what I've learned, French is just one of the many languages she speaks."

"Ah, an occupation which has taken you many places, I'll wager," Daniel exclaimed with the spontaneous delight of one who'd just encountered a kindred spirit. "And you said you lived in France, in Paris perhaps?"

"We lived in a village about a hundred miles from there, but I acquired part of my education in Paris. I know it well." She smiled with fond remembrance. "My mother still lives in our village, so I plan to visit France again later this year." She glanced at Cain who didn't seem to be enjoying the exchange, at all. Why had he interrupted? Was he jealous of Daniel?

"You become more interesting by the minute, *mademoiselle*," Daniel said, his features relaxing into another easy smile. "And I see we'll have much to talk about." He turned again toward his brother. "Where did you find this treasure, Cain?"

"It's a long story," Cain replied in a tone than had taken on a brusque clip. "How long do you intend to be here?"

"As long as it takes to work out some family business," his brother said. Again, he seemed to take no offense at Cain's near rudeness. "Since I was coming anyway, Mother asked me if I could make it home in time for your birthday. I'd counted on staying at least a week or so, but now I think I may stay longer." He glanced at Jade and smiled. "I'd like for us all to get to know each other better."

"I'm sure several people here would like to renew old acquaintances," Cain said, plainly suggesting his brother direct his socializing elsewhere. "I appreciate that you managed to make it home in time for my birthday, Daniel," he amended in a warmer tone. "Have something to eat and enjoy the party. We'll talk later. Right now, I feel the need to dance with my lady."

Cain didn't bother to ask for Jade's permission; he simply took possession of her body and propelled her toward the area cleared for dancing. A smartly dressed redhead had already engaged Daniel in conversation by the time he gathered Jade into his arms and fell in step with the music.

Though Jade didn't understand why exactly, the appearance of his brother had effectively ended her partner's festive mood. He'd seemed friendly toward Daniel—at least part of the exchange had been friendly. Yet a wariness had entered the room along with the older Larkin sibling almost like a second shadow. And the more amiable Daniel had behaved toward her, the more imposing that shadow became. Did Cain feel more threatened than ever by his brother's arrival on the scene? Did he feel so uncertain of her loyalty that he believed his brother might steal her away?

As if he'd read her thoughts, Cain squeezed her to him in a grip so tight she winced and jerked a startled gaze up at him.

"Sorry," he said, relaxing his hold on her a little.

"Cain, what's wrong?" she asked, still holding his gaze. "You seemed to be having such a good time earlier. I thought-well, I thought this party would please you."

"It has pleased me, honey," he was quick to assure her. "I know you and Leona went to a lot of trouble to put it together and I appreciate it."

"Well, something certainly spoiled it for you," she persisted. "Weren't you happy to see your brother?" she ventured cautiously.

"I'd be happier if he *were* my brother." The words seemed to escape Cain's lips unbidden.

"Cain." A pinch of censure mixed with a portion of sympathy in Jade's speaking of his name.

"I'm sorry, I didn't mean to say that," he offered at once. "Daniel's an okay guy. It's just not a very good time for him to visit, that's all."

Jade understood now. She wished Leona had discussed this "special gift" with her before she sprang it on Cain. Already tortured by uncertainty about where he belonged, he hardly needed a reminder that his brother had a rock solid place in the Larkin family. But what assurance could she offer the man she loved that she hadn't replayed with tedious frequency during these past weeks?

Enlisting her actions to speak in place of words, she unclasped her fingers from his and, in defiance of all formal etiquette, pushed both arms around his neck. "I love you," she murmured next to his ear, then wrapped herself around him in a blatant commingling of their bodies. If anyone at the gathering questioned how completely they belonged to each other, her display had to remove all doubt.

"She's a very special woman, all right," Daniel said. Following the intimate dance with Cain, Jade had been hustled off by Leona to assist with some last minute dinner preparations. Her partner had been left alone to visit with his brother. "And from what I've seen and heard," Daniel continued, "she cares for you a lot."

"She's everything wonderful and decent," Cain returned in a defensive tone. "She's all I've ever wanted in a woman."

And she's a lot more than I deserve, he thought guiltily. After all she'd suffered during recent months to protect her integrity, she'd just put it on the line in front of this company of strangers to show how much he meant to her.

"I'm sure she's everything you say," Daniel accepted in his usual quiet tone. "I only meant you look serious about each other."

Cain realized he was being thin-skinned. He couldn't seem to accept anything these days without analyzing it. Daniel wasn't his enemy, but his choosing this time to appear, something didn't feel right about it. What "family" business had been so important he couldn't have conducted it over the phone?

"I figured Leona had told you all about Jade," he said to his brother.

"Mother didn't tell me much. Just that a wonderful young woman had come into your life recently," Daniel said. "And after meeting her, I see how true that is. I couldn't be happier for you, brother."

Was he overreacting? Cain wondered again. Daniel hadn't been part of the Larkins' conspiracy of silence. Still, the timing of his visit troubled. Had his brother been enlisted to seek information about Jade? Or had the Larkins sent him to tell her something?

"She's the best thing that ever came into my life," he confided to his brother. "I'd marry her if I could."

"So, what's stopping you? Go ahead and marry the woman. You don't have anyreason to wait, do you?"

"How can you ask me that, Daniel?" The vehemence in Cain's tone escalated. "You know enough to realize I don't have anything to give her, to give to any woman."

"Does she know, too—about all this?" Daniel asked in the same patient tone.

Cain nodded. "She knows everything I know, which is practically nothing."

"Then, if you love her as she clearly loves you, you have all you need," Daniel argued reasonably. "You don't have to find out about your father to move on with your future. Your life is your own to make what you choose of it."

"Ah, so Leona *has* been talking to you," Cain said, his suspicion rising like bubbles in a pot about to boil. "Don't bother lying about it, Daniel," he cautioned when his brother started to reply. "Here comes Jade. Don't even think about taking her away from me, I warn you," he added, an undisguised threat in his tone. "I won't lose her."

His attention turned to the woman he loved, Cain didn't see the look of sympathetic brotherliness in Daniel's expression. But he did see something else. His senses alert to every nuance of that revealing face, at once he spotted evidence of recent tears in Jade's lustrous eyes. What she'd given to him this evening had cost her dearer than he'd even imagined. He'd never loved her more than now for this latest sacrifice.

And he'd never despised himself more for forcing her to make it.

CHAPTER TEN

"That's it, I've had enough!"

Jade could hardly believe her own voice. She hadn't used language this sharp with Cain since their first meetings. But she despaired daily of her chances against such impossible odds. Cain seemed to punch holes in their relationship faster than she could patch them up.

Dinner with the Larkins tonight had been a disaster. Cain had behaved with such rudeness toward his brother that he'd finally pushed her to the limits of her patience.

Daniel had asked the entire family to gather because he had news he wanted to share. (As usual, it had been a tedious act of persuasion just to get Cain there.) After dessert, his brother had risen, raised his glass, and asked everyone to share in a toast.

"Congratulate me, everyone," he had said, smiling with impish cheer, "I have the best news possible. Georgette Monet has agreed to become my wife."

"Oh, son," Leona burst out. Jade noticed her flustered surprise as she darted a look at Cain then back toward Daniel. "Georgette comes from such an important family with so much concern about pedigree." At once seeming to realize the implication of her remarks, she smoothed them over with, "But that's wonderful news, Daniel, you've chosen a lovely girl. You must tell us how you finally convinced her to consent."

Daniel, who hadn't seemed to notice anything out of turn, proceeded to explain how he'd persuaded his fiancee to accept his proposal. As it turned out, the only reason for her reluctance was the physical distance between their families. Soon everyone at the table was congratulating Cain's brother—everyone, that is, except Cain. From the way he'd behaved, Jade wondered whether he actually resented his sibling's happiness. Now that the natural child of the Larkins had reaffirmed his place as the son and heir, did Cain interpret it as a final act of ostracism?

"I said I've had enough of this!" Jade repeated with even more emphasis to her sullen companion.

"What-what do you mean?" Pulled back finally from whatever dark place he retreated to these days, he finally seemed to realize what she'd said. They were alone on the rear veranda. The rest of the family had drifted into the living room, and she heard the sound of a familiar French tune being played on the piano. She would have enjoyed talking more with Daniel about the woman he'd chosen for his wife, but, as usual, she had appeased Cain's ill humor and followed him out onto the porch. This was the first sign that he was even aware of her presence. "What are you talking about?"

"I'm talking about your behavior, of course," she said in exasperation. "Why didn't you join in with congratulating Daniel tonight?" she pressed before she lost his attention again. "He has a right to marry if he's found the right woman. Why should he have to put his life on hold because you choose to?"

She realized that last remark had stung so she didn't pursue it. Instead, she continued with the reasons for her frustration, "It isn't just Daniel, although I'd hoped his being here might help you loosen up with your family. But by the end of the evening, you seemed annoyed with everything and everyone—including me. What have I done to displease you?'

"Nothing. I just—"

"You were glowering at all of us," she interrupted, no longer willing to be put off by his denials. "You'd think we had committed some sin because we dared to display our good humor in front of you.

"I said I've had enough, Cain." The finality in her own voice startled her. "And I meant it. I was willing to wait for us to get married, even more willing to marry you without ever knowing anything about your background. But every day since you've set out on this quest, your dark moods have gotten longer. And now with your brother's arrival, you've not only shut yourself off from your family, but you seem to want to shut me off, as well."

"You've all been so busy discovering everything you have in common," he flared, "I'm surprised you've even noticed how I behaved."

Jade stopped herself from voicing a retort, although she could think of several. This remark was merely a reflection of Cain's latest paranoia. Anytime she spent even a few minutes with the rest of his family, he seemed to suspect some conspiracy. She'd assured him with agonizing frequency that she meant only to make Daniel feel welcome. Yet at the next opportunity, he'd leapt to more erroneous conclusions. Lovemaking had become an almost desperate act, as though Cain had to prove over and over that she belonged to him.

And she'd never liked the idea of being anyone's possession.

She closed her eyes and breathed out a weighted sigh before she said, "I'm through arguing the point with you, Cain. Clearly, it's useless." She crossed to the lounge chair and picked up her jacket. "Will you take me home, please?"

Cain's look of annoyance subsided into one of confusion. "Why don't you stay awhile and talk," he ventured. "We can go for a walk if you feel restless."

She shook her head. "I'm not the one who's restless. I wouldn't mind doing whatever you wanted—as long as you acted as if you enjoyed having me with you."

One dark eyebrow arched inquisitively. "I always enjoy having you with me."

"You don't enjoy anything anymore, Cain," she contradicted. "You've become so tangled up in this latest obsession you've stopped living your life entirely."

The arched eyebrow lowered and pinched together with the other. Cain opened his mouth to speak, then closed it again without voicing whatever he'd meant to say.

"Let's go," he said simply. Lapsing into silence, he helped her with her jacket and accompanied her across the side lawn to the place where his car was parked.

The interior of Cain's Lincoln contained all the warmth of a drafty igloo. Neither occupant said a word or made a move toward the other during their drive to Jade's apartment.

Only when she reached to unlock her front door did Cain speak again. "Look, I apologize *again* for being so uptight lately. Let's go inside and sit for a few minutes, maybe have a drink and just talk."

Jade shook her head. "I don't feel like talking any more tonight, Cain. I have to go to work tomorrow and I'm tired."

He seemed to contemplate persuading her, then to think better of it. "All right, we'll call it a night if you want. I'll pick you up after work tomorrow."

She stood with her back pressed against the door. Somehow, she needed the solidness of the wood to support her while she spoke. "You expect me to spend another evening with you? Why? So I can sit by and watch you turn into an iceman in front of your family again, to remain helpless while you introduce a chill into everyone's evening? Or maybe I can look forward to spending hours more exiled in some corner with you, watching you brood while the others are having a good time? I don't think so. You don't get it, Cain. I'm tired of spending our time together this way. *I have had enough.*"

"All right," he said, "we'll leave my family to visit on their own and go to dinner somewhere by ourselves."

"That's no solution. It'll only look as if we're trying to avoid Daniel. No, Cain. Your brother has said he can spare only a short time to visit. You should be with him as much as possible while he's here."

An angry shadow fell over Cain's features again. "Are you suggesting we not see each other at all while my brother's in town?"

"What I'm suggesting is that you think about rejoining your family because I can't continue any longer with things the way they are. It's just too hard."

When Cain didn't answer, Jade realized the futility of continuing the conversation. "Look, I'm too tired to go on with this right now," she said with a sigh. "And I have things to do before I turn in. Let's talk about it after you've had time to think about what I've said."

"I'll call you tomorrow," he countered, still stubbornly refusing to recognize her point. Before she had time to resist, he clenched his fingers into her hair and forced her to him. "I will not lose you," he said, his statement sounding as much like a vow to himself as a promise to her. Then his mouth smashed onto hers in what had become a familiar stamp of possession.

She didn't try to break away. She parted her lips freely and allowed him to explore and stake his claim. But when he tore himself away at last amid struggling gasps for air, she deftly slipped from his embrace. She twisted the doorknob behind her and, with a whispered, "Good night, Cain," she evaporated inside the slightly open door.

Cain stood for minutes and contemplated the door which Jade had virtually shut in his face. He wanted to force it open, to crush her in his arms and kiss her until neither of them could bear another second without making love.

But he wouldn't do any of those things—not tonight. She was tired and cross. And she had a right to be. She had spoken the truth. Each time something intensified his insecurities, he'd forced her to endure another of his dark moods. He realized she'd done her best always to understand. But how could she comprehend that this secretiveness about his origins hung like the rotting mist over the House of Usher in Poe's dark tale of another family's curse?

And now with this sudden appearance of Daniel, what else was going on that he wasn't being told about? The Larkins had excluded him from their "family" meetings.

Had they talked only about business, or had something relating to Jade and him entered into their discussions?

"No!" he gritted, "I will not lose her, too."

Angry and despondent, he turned away from Jade's door and walked down the steps to his SUV. He'd leave her alone tonight and allow her to get her rest. Tomorrow they'd make up, and he'd promise her that from now on no dark moods would spoil their time together (and he'd try his best this time to keep that promise). He turned the ignition key and the powerful engine purred to life.

Yes, tomorrow, he vowed, tomorrow he'd make everything all right again.

Jade put down her red pencil and arranged the homework papers from her language classes in a neat pile on her desk. She felt more tired than she had last night. She'd gone to bed at a reasonable hour, but she had barely slept. How long was she expected to endure the strain of this complicated relationship with Cain? She was sure Cy and Leona had meant just the opposite to happen, but their inviting Daniel here at this time had only increased their other son's feelings of estrangement. Family gatherings had become the scene of one confrontation after another. And she didn't think she could stand being in the middle any longer.

Cain would call, of course he would. His overwhelming need to keep her near had somehow become mixed up with this obsession about his family history. As the threat weighed more heavily on his mind that he might lose her, his need to hold onto her grew more desperate.

Though she didn't know how to help him anymore, still, her heart ached for him every time she witnessed his pain. She loved him so much. And she knew that love, weighted down by guilt for not being able to hold out as she'd promised, would crumble her resistance, and she'd give in to him when he phoned.

Even now, guilt nudged at her to call him herself. For her own survival, she must seek a way to ward off this feeling. Amy Dunne, one of the engineers in her Russian class, had asked her to go shopping this evening. Initially, she'd meant to refuse. But perhaps she should go, after all.

The two women had developed a friendship over the past few weeks. Amy was a dark-haired beauty with a figure suited to the latest fashions. Her friend had already introduced her to many of the great little shops where she bought her own smartly tailored clothes. Witty and fun loving, Amy had brightened some very gloomy days lately with her on-going appraisal of the male population at work. Her friend might be just the tonic she needed to fortify her drained spirits.

Jade picked up the phone and dialed Amy's office number. "I deserve a little time for me," she offered aloud to excuse herself. "and this once I'm going to take it."

"What do you think of that one?"

Prompted by her friend's comment, Jade glanced out the window of the quaint little tea room where they'd stopped for a light supper. Several times during the past few minutes, Amy had made an effort to engage her in a favorite pastime—rating the sexiness of the derrieres of each of the males who passed outside. This girls-night-out had, as Jade had hoped, provided her with a spontaneous respite from her troubles with Cain. She was actually having a good time, the best she'd enjoyed in weeks. A fashion fanatic, Amy had dragged her through half the boutiques in Atlanta, it seemed. Unfortunately, her mind now released from having to decide among the latest fashion fads, she felt herself slipping again into troublesome thoughts about Cain.

She looked at Amy and forced a chuckle. "Not my type. His jeans are a little too tight and that behind wasn't made for showing off."

Amy laughed. A second later, however, she abandoned her amusing pastime to stare openly at Jade. Her mischievous grin faded into a look of concern.

"Okay, give, kiddo," she scolded mildly. "I've been trying to win over your attention for the past five minutes without success. We were having a good time earlier, but the minute we sat down here, you began to drift off on me. It's can't be me since I'm such an entertaining person." She chuckled briefly then grew serious again. "So, let's have it, girlfriend, what's bothering you?"

Jade jerked her attention from absently counting the rosebuds on her China cup to stare back at her friend. "Nothing, Amy, I'm fine, really."

"Now, don't you look at me with those big, beautiful eyes and tell me that," Amy snorted. "Lying isn't something you're good at. You

my brother these past few days and when I have, you haven't been with him. He hasn't said where you were, nothing. I'd gotten worried that he might be on the verge of losing you."

"I haven't broken off my relationship with Cain," Jade confided. Glad that she could tell him the truth, at least on that point, she went on to explain, "I have let work keep me away a little more than was absolutely necessary, but I had a reason. I'd hoped that, by stepping away for awhile, I might take some of the pressure off everybody. Lately, whenever I've spoken to another member of your family, Cain seems to think that, well, that—"

"That we're hatching some conspiracy," Daniel finished for her.

Her eyes widened in surprise at his frank appraisal. "But no one is conspiring behind his back—are you?"

"Of course not. At least, not in the way he thinks. I realize now that bringing up my marriage plans was the wrong thing to do. Mother saw it at once, but she couldn't warn me to shut up in time. I suppose I should have realized beforehand that now was perhaps the worst time in the world to announce that I was getting married. The way Cain's been feeling lately, it must have seemed like another slap in the face to him."

"I think it did, but that wasn't your fault. You had a right to share your happy news with your family. But while we're on that subject, something's bothered me, too—you remember Leona's remark about your fiancee's family?"

He nodded. "The fact that I didn't see that one coming makes me twice the idiot.You see, Georgette comes from a very old, very prestigious family in Quebec. They have a strong sense of family history and honor. I've been kicking myself for not realizing that my making such a big deal about a family with a respected genealogy must have been another cruel reminder to Cain of the uncertainties in his own background. And those uncertainties are what's keeping him from grabbing on to a future with you."

She nodded. "He's really fixated on the possibility that something awful surrounds his family's history, isn't he? Do you know anything about it?"

Daniel shook his head. “Believe it or not, Mother and Dad have told me next to nothing about how they got Cain. Which has always been fine with me, he’s my brother, I love him. But,” he continued with a sigh, “this obsession to know the truth about his family, at the same time dreading what he might find out, has taken him over so completely, he’s afraid to live, at all, anymore. I know he loves you, but he can’t bring himself to ask a woman like you to share her life to him. I’ve been worried that you were beginning to feel the same way.”

“It’s not that I’m afraid of anything he might learn,” she was quick to protest, “it’s just that-well, I can’t seem to make him realize it doesn’t matter; I’d love him, anyway. I don’t know what else to do to help him.”

Daniel nodded his understanding. “I’d hoped I might have found a way.” When her gaze became questioning, “I said a minute ago I wasn’t conspiring with my parents against Cain,” he explained. “What we have been attempting to do is locate his father and perhaps convince him to talk to his son.”

Jade perked up at that. “Oh, Daniel, if only you could make that happen. It might give Cain exactly the closure he needs. Have you had any luck yet?”

“Mother tells me her brother checks in with a lawyer here in the city from time to time,” Daniel confided. “But there’s no pattern to it. We’ve been able to convince the lawyer to relay the urgency of our request, but we’ve had no word yet about it.”

“Oh, Daniel,” Jade said, her breath diffusing in a sigh, “I don’t think I can take much more of this waiting. And we both know what it’s doing to Cain. One of these people just has to tell us something soon.”

“These people?” Daniel questioned, picking up on her reference. “Is someone else working to find Cain’s father?”

For long seconds, Jade didn’t answer. Daniel’s loving concern had won her trust so completely she’d forgotten another trust she’d promised to protect. Now her careless slip had snagged her with a fresh dilemma. If she let Daniel in on any of the information she’d agreed to keep silent about, wouldn’t it be a double betrayal?

"Ever since Cain and I have become serious enough to be talking about marriage." she ventured, "he's become more determined than ever to locate his biological family. I'd hoped I might help by pressing Cy and Leona for information. If they felt they couldn't share anything, I thought they might, at least, give me some advice about what I should do. Heaven knows, waiting wasn't doing anyone any good."

Daniel looked slightly startled. "And did my parents tell you something more about all this?"

She nodded. "A little of it. They explained that if they told Cain about his father or passed along the information to anyone who then told him, they would forfeit all monies they'd received when they took him in as a boy."

"Uh-huh." His eyes still intent on hers, Daniel rubbed his chin pensively. "Of course, I know about the financial arrangements. My parents told me a long time ago and, naturally, they made me swear never to tell anyone. I've always felt burdened with even that little bit of information, just as I'm guessing you do. I'm not surprised they took you into their confidence, though. You have to believe they've only acted out of love for both Cain and me."

"Of course I see that," Jade was quick to reply. "I know they're good people."

With the thoroughness of a jeweler's loupe, his pale eyes bored into her deep green ones. "There's something else you haven't told me, isn't there, Jade?" he asked finally.

Impaled by his scrutinous gaze, she quickly sifted her brain for all she knew about Daniel. Did he care more about his brother than his inheritance? Her heart told her he did.

"Cain has hired a private detective," she blurted out in a rush. "He thinks a professional may have better luck with tracing his family."

"Uh-oh." Daniel contemplated her revelation for seconds, but his look indicated concern, not apprehension. "I don't know whether that was a wise thing to do or not," he reasoned aloud. "It may hurt our parents if they find out. But maybe Cain had done the only thing he could do, after all. I hope it pays off for him."

"Have you been told any more about his father yourself?" she had to know. "Perhaps why he left the country?"

"No, not really. I think the man must have been in serious trouble, though, to have abandoned his son. Mother says he doted on the boy. But even if I'd learned the trouble that drove his father away was something criminal, it wouldn't have changed my feelings for Cain. I've loved him like a blood brother ever since he came to live with us."

Jade breathed out a sigh of relief. She'd judged Daniel Larkin correctly. "I've told Cain the same thing over and over again. I just wish he'd believe it and give up on all this."

A smile brightened Daniel's features. "Bless you, Jade. I knew you were the perfect woman for Cain." He reached out and squeezed her hand with brotherly affection. "It'll work out all right. We just have to keep telling ourselves that."

The shrill interruption of the phone quelled his reassuring words. "Excuse me."

Jade said, turning to answer it.

"Is Daniel still there?" Leona's immediate and almost hysterical question alarmed Jade. "May I speak to him, please?" she continued before Jade could respond.

Sensing the urgency of Leona's plea, she handed the receiver to Daniel without questions of her own. "Your mother," she said simply.

After a brief and very agitated conversation, Daniel hung up the phone and turned to Jade. The look on his face increased her alarm even before he spoke.

"Cain just left my parents' house in such a state Mother thought she ought to warn us," he said. "He's found out, Jade. He knows everything."

CHAPTER ELEVEN

"You'd better leave, Daniel."

Considering the seriousness of his revelation, Jade realized the presence of Cain's foster brother in her apartment would only make a potentially volatile situation worse. Apparently, Cain had received some news, likely news of the worst kind.

"My brother already knows I'm here," Daniel said. "In any case, I wouldn't leave you here alone with him."

"I'm not afraid of Cain, Daniel."

Cain's foster brother reached out and took both her hands in his. Apprehension mixed with concern in his gaze, he started in measured tones, "Look, Jade, I know Cain loves you, but he's wild with anger and grief right now. There's no telling what he might do. Mother says he's already forced her and Dad to admit they've always known the details of his father's disappearance. He's convinced we've all conspired to keep it from him."

Suddenly, Jade understood the reason for Daniel's concern. "Oh, dear Lord! You mean he thinks I'm part of that conspiracy?"

Daniel nodded. "I'm afraid so." His features contorted into a look of pained sympathy. "And I haven't told you the worst of it yet."

"What? What haven't you told me?" she asked, more panicked than before.

Daniel hesitated again before he spoke. "Cain's not thinking straight, Jade. Since you've been making excuses not to see him the past few days, he's gotten it into his head that you've already been told everything about his family. And because of what you've learned, you've changed your mind about marrying him."

Jade felt the strength drain from her limbs. "Oh, no," she murmured, "he thinks I've abandoned him, too." A steadying arm caught her when she swayed on her feet.

"Perhaps you'd better lie down," Daniel suggested with heightened concern as he helped her to the sofa. "Let me talk to Cain."

"No, oh no, Daniel, I can't," she objected at once. Silently, she prayed that the courage which had sustained her in the past would hold together now. "The last thing I want to do right now is hide from him. Somehow I have to convince him how wrong he is. Whatever he's found out about his family, it doesn't matter. I love him. Oh, Daniel, I—"

As if a gust of wind had jerked it from its fastenings, the front door suddenly burst open. In a single motion, Daniel and Jade snapped attention toward the sound. Jade hardly recognized the figure looming in the open portal. His carelessly loosened tie and unbuttoned collar suggested a person who could barely stand the feel of his own clothing. An obvious consequence of the repeated tortures of nervous fingers, his hair dangled in unkempt strands over his furrowed brow. The veins in his neck and face stood out like guy wires securing his tight features.

"Cain!" Jade cried out. Leaping up from the sofa, she hurried across the room toward him. Daniel was right behind her. "Oh, Cain, we've been so worried about you." she said, automatically reaching out to comfort him. Her gesture fell on empty air, however, when he stepped back out of her reach.

"I might have known Daniel would have come here," he shot at her in angry retort. "With more conspiring in mind, no doubt."

"Daniel didn't come here to conspire against you." She tried without success to keep her voice calm. "He just came over to—"

"Tell me, Jade," Cain bit out, interrupting her denial, "how did it feel when you learned the whole story about my sordid past? A woman with your tender sensibilities, it must have boggled to learn how justified my fears have been. Let me guess," he went on before she could contradict this latest indictment, "what was it that finally pushed you to find out the whole nasty truth? Was it all my talk about that painting? Or maybe what I told you about Cy and Leona's behavior made you suspicious?" His eyes dropped as he delivered the final crashing blow. "Well, now you know it all, Jade. What decent family would offer their name to the son of a man who murdered his own brother?"

The enormity of Cain's revelation so astounded Jade she couldn't have spoken then if her life had depended on it. Thankfully, Daniel stepped in to make a reply.

"Cain, I don't know what you're talking about, and neither does Jade. But it wouldn't matter if we did. Don't you see, none of your past matters. We—"

"Doesn't matter?" Cain's bloodshot eyes shot up, impaling his brother this time. His lip curled into another derisive sneer. "How could it not matter that my father left the country before he could be arrested for murder? That he dragged me along with him, then dumped me at his stepsister's door like excess baggage when he decided I was becoming too much of a liability?"

When Jade came to herself finally, she took another step toward Cain, arms open in supplication. "Listen to what Daniel is saying," she pleaded. "None of this matters. Any trouble your father might have had happened a long time ago. He may have been guilty of something awful. Who knows? But whatever he did has nothing to do with you now." She reached out to touch the man she loved, but, as before, he jerked away from her. A second later, he commenced another round of verbal blows aimed at his brother.

"Why the hell didn't you have the decency to tell me, Daniel?" he demanded. "Or had Cy and Leona warned you not to break the bargain they'd made with my father? Did your share of their little empire mean so much to you, too, that you wouldn't risk losing it for my sake?"

With a single lightning stroke, Cain reached out and grabbed his brother by the shirt collar. "What's the matter, Daniel?" he gritted, glaring into his sibling's startled eyes. "Are you worried I might do something to ruin your marriage to your noble lady? Afraid now that I've lost everything important to me, I might turn into what my father was?" Cain's grip tightened. "Is that it, you think what happened before might happen aga—?

"Oh, my God!" Suddenly, the angry color drained from Cain's face. Eyes darting from his brother to Jade, he murmured, "what am I doing?" His voice died away and he stared mutely at her anguished features. Then his fingers uncurled from Daniel's shirt collar, and his arms dropped listlessly to his sides. "I'm sorry, Daniel," he got out in a strained whisper. Then, without another word, he turned and disappeared out the door.

Minutes passed before Jade regained her senses. Turning anxious eyes toward Daniel, "Are you okay?" she asked finally.

Daniel nodded. "I'm okay—but Cain…"

"I have to go after him," she said, mouthing their equal concern, "Somehow, I have to make him listen."

"Wait a minute, Jade," Daniel cautioned, catching her arm when she started for the door, "we need to think about this first. You don't know what—"

Is everything all right?" Preceding her husband through the open front door, Leona Larkin peered anxiously into the room. "Oh, thank God," she sighed when she saw both young people. Automatically, her arms outstretched to embrace them. "After Cain left us, we didn't know what might happen."

"Where is he?" Cy injected. His countenance betrayed equal relief that they were unharmed. "Did he cause any trouble?"

"Cain has been here and gone," Daniel furnished. "He made a lot of wild accusations, but he hasn't harmed anyone but himself. Jade wants to go after him, and I've been trying to convince her not to."

"I've got to find him and talk to him," Jade anguished aloud. "I have to try to help him get through this. He's hurting."

"I know he's hurting," Daniel said sympathetically. "But we have to find out more about this whole situation first." He turned again to his parents and gestured toward the sofa. "Mom, Dad, you have to tell Jade and me the whole story—and quickly."

Cy and Leona Larkin looked at one another. For a moment, they stared in silent communication. Then they seated themselves side by side on the sofa. Hurriedly, Jade and Daniel took seats in the chairs opposite.

"First, we want to apologize to you, Jade," Leona spoke up. "We should have told you the whole story when you asked us earlier."

"We need your forgiveness, too, son," Cy offered to Daniel in amendment. "We realize now we should have told you everything years ago instead of a few bits and pieces. We thought we could spare both our sons by keeping the truth from you."

Jade leaned forward in her chair. "Then, whoever inherited the business has never been you main concern?" she guessed.

"No," The couple chorused in unison. "If we'd decided it was the best thing to do," Leona added, "no sacrifice, not even the loss of our business, would have prevented us from telling the whole truth."

Daniel reached out and patted his mother's hand. "And I would have supported any decision you made without hesitation," he said. "Now, tell us what's going on. What do you know that you haven't shared with us? And what does Cain think he knows?"

"Cain's father is Delancy Morgan," Leona revealed at the start. "He's my stepbrother, as I said. Del named his son after him. We had to change the boy's name when we took him in, though. We didn't want to invite questions from prying news people when we returned to America. As far as everyone but Del's lawyer knew, the child was our own second son born while we were overseas. We called him Cain because it was my maiden name. We decided to hide Delancy as his middle name, hoping no one at home would make the connection to my stepbrother but leaving a door open if Del could ever come back and reclaim all that was his."

"So, how was Cain able to find out about his birth father?" Jade prompted.

"That private detective he hired recently traced us back to France," Cy explained. "We were living there when Del came to us with his troubles. He knew we'd planned to leave the country in a month or two to return to America. He thought we could get his child back home without much trouble, and, as it turned out, we did."

"The authorities didn't question you about him?" Jade asked.

Cy shook his head. "Not much. The story we told was that Cain had been left with us by my brother, an American soldier, who had fathered the child by a French girl now dead. The government officials didn't seem to care; they just gave us the papers to take the boy with us. I guess the way they looked at it, there was no record of him being missing. If we accepted the responsibility, they'd have one less foreigner's waif to burden their system."

"But what's all this about Cain's father being a criminal?" Daniel asked. "Is it true?"

"Del was in trouble when he came to us in France," Leona took up in explanation. "Bad trouble. That private detective must have played around with the names of our family members until he located the newspaper accounts of the murder."

"Murder?" Jade demanded. "Whose murder?"

"Wait, let her explain," Daniel soothed. "Mother?"

"Maybe it'd be better if I started from the beginning," Leona continued. "Del was a struggling young artist when he married Cain's mother. She was a handsome woman, older than he was, I think. I doubt if she ever loved him, but his youth and talent intrigued her for a time. With a small legacy his own father left him, Del bought the gallery to support his new wife. But he was always wandering off to paint, and he didn't devote enough time building up the gallery to suit her demands for money. She certainly wasn't willing to starve with him while he tried to sell his own paintings. Soon after their son was born, she took up with another man and ran off with him.

"Unfortunately, the tragedies in Del's life had just started. He and my other stepbrother Louis never got along. Louis was a ruthless businessman. He criticized Del constantly about wasting his time with what he called a worthless hobby."

"You've never talked about either of your stepbrothers," Daniel inserted. "I thought you had no family left."

"I know, son," Leona said apologetically. "It was impossible to tell you about my brothers without explaining all this other."

He nodded. "I understand. Go on, Mother."

"Well, Louis' bullying finally convinced Del that he wasn't doing right by his son by continuing to paint. So, from then on he concentrated on making the gallery pay. It was ironic; while Del's business was beginning to make money, Louis' was going downhill." Daniel's mother glanced over at her husband and sighed heavily. His nodding encouragement seemed to give her the impetus to go on.

"I think my older brother completely lost his reasoning after that. Everything became a competition, even his private life. Since Del's marriage had failed, Louis was determined to show him up by acquiring a wife of his own. He returned one day from a business trip to New Orleans bragging about the beauty he'd married. We never met the girl, but Del described her to us." The older woman paused to stare poignantly at Jade, as though she wanted to say something else but didn't know how. "The way Louis treated his wife," she went on finally, "Del said she was like his slave.

"I can't tell you she remained faithful to him. Del swore she tried to make the marriage work. I know the two of them made a deadly mistake when they became friends. By this time, Del had hired a good manager for his gallery so he could start back creating his own paintings, and he persuaded his sister-in-law to pose for him. Louis went crazy when he found out. He was sure the two of them were using the painting sessions to cover an affair. One of their meeting spots was a cabin that used to stand on the property we later gave to Cain."

"So that land wasn't really part of his legacy from his father?" Jade questioned.

"Not exactly," Leona answered. "It belonged to our whole family, but since Del was gone…Cy and I thought if we gave it to Cain, he would feel he had something that was truly his. Of course, we all used the place back in those days for weekend camping trips. Del's meetings with his brother's wife were probably innocent enough. I understand the boy usually came with them."

That explained why the property seemed so familiar to Cain, Jade thought, but she didn't interrupt.

"Events came to a horrible climax right there at the cabin," Leona said. "Three people destroyed one another.

"Del had gone there alone the day it happened. Earlier that morning, Louis had finally realized his business was bankrupt, and he took out his frustrations on his wife the way he usually did, with verbal and then physical abuse. He called her awful names, all with the same ugly meaning—adulteress. He forced her tell him where she'd been meeting Del, and, when she did, he beat her even more until she fell unconscious. Then he got in his car and took off for the cabin to have it out with his brother."

"But you said three people were at the cabin," Jade reminded her.

Leona nodded. "As it was explained to us, the girl regained her senses soon after Louis left her. She managed to get to her car and follow him. When she arrived at the cabin, Louis was in the midst of a savage attack on Del. But when he saw what Louis had done to his wife's face, adrenalin must have kicked in. He lunged at Louis like a madman and beat him senseless. Del wanted the girl to leave then with him. It had to have been obvious that she needed a doctor. But she wouldn't go. She said she had to stay and take care of her husband.

"I guess Louis never regained consciousness. It's unclear what happened during those last hours. The following morning Del learned the cabin had burned with Louis and his wife trapped inside. The two men had knocked over an oil stove during the fight, Del said. He could only guess that that's what destroyed the cabin. The rescuers found Louis dead at the scene. Del heard a few days later that the girl had died at a local hospital."

"But who did that leave to explain what really happened?" Jade had to know.

"No one really," Leona said. "All the evidence against Del was circumstantial, but he had no defense. Since Louis' housekeeper had overheard his accusations of adultery against his wife, naturally, the police concluded that she and Del had conspired to kill her husband. They figured Kellus had simply gotten caught in her own trap."

Kellus? The name struck Jade like a fist to her midsection. Her mother. Was that what Leona hadn't had the courage to mention a few minutes ago? But Leona had said the woman died. Even discounting that information, her mother had no burn marks, no scars of any kind, on her face.

Her father, of course! He had possessed the skills to repair a broken face, a face that had once looked just like hers. Her mother *was* the woman in the painting. No wonder Cain had been so certain that she knew everything. Her senses reeled from the impact of self-revelation.

"But Del Morgan was never arrested and prosecuted?" Daniel spoke up, filling the void of silence.

"No, they never found him," Cy offered in reply. "Del left the United States before he could be charged with any crime. As soon as he heard the news that Kellus was dead, he had no reason to stay. So he got together all the cash he could put his hands on, instructed his lawyer to turn over power of attorney to his friend Lawrence Collier so his property could be taken care of and escaped to France with his son."

"And came to us," Leona resumed. "We were just a young family struggling to build up our import business." She offered her son a weak smile. "You were barely four at the time, Daniel, so you wouldn't remember. We'd been living in Paris temporarily to establish business contacts in Europe. Del explained the hopelessness of his situation and begged us to take his son and raise him."

"I do remember when Cain came to live with us," Daniel said. "I was thrilled to be getting a brother."

Leona nodded. "We were all happy to have the boy, even though the circumstances were so unhappy. Of course, we did accept the financial arrangement Del offered us," she said, turning to Jade. "He insisted and it helped us over some rough times. But we would have taken Cain without it and adopted him. But that's not what Del wanted. He didn't know when he might be able to return for his child, but he said he couldn't let him go completely. That made adoption impossible, of course, so we agreed to take Cain according to the terms we explained to you, Jade. We've tried to honor our agreement with my stepbrother and insure his son an inheritance, but we could never explain things without telling him the whole truth."

"But what you did tell me was the truth, wasn't it?" Jade asked when she'd managed to restore some of her composure. "Del Morgan refused to give up his son for good, and that's how you became locked into this peculiar agreement?"

Leona nodded. "No one in Atlanta knew I was Del's stepsister except Lawrence Collier. Thank goodness, the media never dug deeply enough to discover our connection. When we moved back to Atlanta a few months after Cain was left with us, nobody questioned that both boys were our own sons. That's the whole story as far as we know it." She reached out and patted Jade's hand. "I'm so sorry for the pain all of us have caused you, my dear."

Jade squeezed the older woman's hand. She saw sympathy in Leona's features and realized her face telegraphed her own pain. Did Leona Larkin attribute her stricken appearance merely to anxiety over Cain? Or had she guessed about Kellus, as well?

"I understand you've tried recently to locate Cain's father yourselves?" she solicited, including both the Larkins in her questioning gaze.

"Oh, yes, for months now," Leona affirmed. "We'd hoped he might be willing to speak to Cain now and somehow explain his absence. I'm so sorry we couldn't manage a reunion before Cain found out the facts this way."

"I'm grateful to you both for sharing this with me," Jade said after a few minutes of pensive silence. "But I still have to talk to Cain."

"You don't even know where he went," Leona argued.

"I know where he'll go eventually," Jade replied with absolute certainty.

"What can you say to him?" Daniel asked.

"I don't know exactly," she admitted. "I only know I have to try to make him believe none of us betrayed him, that he is, and always has been, loved unconditionally."

Daniel pushed a weak smile onto his lips and nodded. "You're quite a woman, Jade Hartman. Good luck to you. I hope you can persuade Cain to believe you—for both your sakes."

Cain stood in front of his desk, a knife in his hand poised to strike. His cottage looked as if warring armies had fired cannonballs into it. Tattered fragments of the detective's report lay strewn on the floor. His own plans for the gallery annex clung in awkward suspension off one edge of the drafting table. The remains of the canvases he now knew for certain his father had painted lay like mutilated soldiers on a battlefield.

Cain gripped the knife to continue his devastation when his rabid gaze snagged on something. It was the photograph he'd taken of Jade that day the two of them picnicked in the country. He froze statue-still, his eyes fixed hypnotically on her face. Unnoticed, the weapon slipped from his fingers and landed on the floor with a hollow thud.

Had it all been a lie? All these weeks, had he deluded himself that some unknown force had transformed a portrait into a living, breathing woman? A woman who was not only beautiful, but warm and loving—and in love with him?

"No!" burst from his lips, his agonized cry echoing throughout the room. She *had* loved him, for a while at least. She'd accepted the impermanence of their relationship. She'd even held fast during his dark moods, always with the belief that eventually they would have a future together. Only after she'd learned the whole truth had she been unable to bear it any longer. How could he blame her from backing away from such ugliness? Why would such a perfect treasure want to attach herself to a piece of base metal like him?

With the tenderness of a father caressing his sleeping child, Cain touched the glossy likeness of the woman he loved. He couldn't destroy this photograph of her. For a little while she had been his. But only in a picture could one make love last forever.

Jade slipped quietly through the partially open door of the cottage. His eyes riveted to the photograph he held in his hand, Cain didn't notice her approach.

"Cain?" she ventured, stopping a few feet away from him.

He seemed startled and, for a second, his eyes bored into the static image in front of him. Only after she spoke his name a second time did his head whip around to stare into her animated features. A look of longing shadowed across his visage, but it darkened quickly into anger.

"Why have you come here, Jade?" he demanded.

"Because we mustn't leave things this way," she answered softly.

He raised his hand in a gesture of dismissal. "Since these 'things' can't be changed, they're better left alone. Surely, you've realized that."

"You really don't believe that."

"Don't I? What do you want from me, Jade? You want me to plead with you to forget that I'm the spawn of a murderer? My roots are grounded in the same bloody soil as the first man who lifted a hand against his own brother. Do you think I could ask you to accept the name of a family like that?

"Cy and Leona couldn't bring themselves to make me their son," he continued, furnishing her with no opportunity to answer. "I can't hold that against them any longer; why should they want the taint of my father's sins on their family name? I couldn't expect anyone decent to take on such a burden." As though it had become too difficult to look into her face any longer, he turned away and walked to the window. "Go away, Jade," he said without twisting his head. "You've already made the right decision. You're better off without me."

"I don't want to leave, Cain," she said in a voice lifted in supplication. "Please, I want to stay with you."

He made a scoffing sound and continued to stare blindly out the window.

"It's true," she insisted. "None of what's happened changes anything between us, not as far as I'm concerned."

"And I suppose you expect me to believe you haven't already been avoiding me these past few nights?" Though he still didn't look at her, his tone indicated he considered the question rhetorical.

"I was busy those nights, just as I told you," she hedged, knowing she had no chance of explaining the reasons for her absence to Cain now. "I went shopping with a girlfriend one evening, and the other two nights I attended the company parties I told you about."

"Next you'll be telling me you hadn't already learned about my family's history."

She heard in his voice the same disdain as before.

"No, I won't tell you that. I did know—at least some of it."

Clearly startled that she'd admitted it so readily, he turned and faced her again.

"And yet you didn't say anything to me? You just held on to your little secrets and let me continue to squirm?"

"Cain, it wasn't that way," she said, her voice now a plea for understanding. "I did pressure your parents to explain to me why they'd never adopted you. They finally told me about your father being forced to leave the country. I knew he must have had some kind of trouble, but the Larkins never revealed what it was. I only know he asked them to care for you but firmly rejected their offer to adopt you.

"That, I promise, is all I knew before today. Maybe I should have shared it with you, but I gave the Larkins my word I wouldn't. I didn't gain any more information until today when Cy and Leona told me—and Daniel—the rest of the story."

"What a cozy little gathering that must have been," he hissed. "Too bad your mother couldn't have been there."

"My mother—?"

"Of course. Talking to her put you on the trail of the story in the first place, didn't it? Clever lady. She's changed a great deal. That threw me off. I thought I'd made a mistake, that your looking like her portrait really was just a coincidence.

"I guess the fire must have damaged her face pretty badly. Cosmetic surgery can certainly cover a multitude of sins. I still wonder how she faked her own death." He stared at Jade a moment, as though he saw another face in hers. "She was a beautiful woman, your mother. I suppose that's why my father thought she was worth committing murder for."

Jade's head jerked backward, the impact of Cain's words as stinging as a slap across the face. "I spoke to my mother, I admit that," she said when she found her voice again. "But she denied knowing anything about your family and I didn't press it. I only guessed minutes ago when the Larkins told us the whole story that *Maman* must have had reconstructive surgery, and that's why her face is so changed. My father was a brilliant surgeon, and he loved her very much. But I swear I never knew she'd been his patient. I didn't even know she'd been married before to Louis Morgan."

"Very good, Jade." He clapped his hands in mock applause, "a well-rehearsed speech, I must say." Another sneer accompanied his derisive remark. "I see you've learned to put together lies with a brilliance matched only by the Larkins."

Hot tears pushed at Jade's eyelids in response to his merciless assault. When she spoke this time, her voice shook perceptibly. "Cain, I don't know what happened between my mother and your father. Neither of us has heard their side of it yet. All I know is, it doesn't matter. I love you, and at least four other people do, too. "Yes, four," she affirmed, cutting short the argument she saw about to form on his lips, "your father, whatever his mistakes, tried to provide for you the best way he could. And that's all you should remember about him. He's paid for whatever crimes he committed with the sacrifice of everything that meant anything to him.

"I don't think we have the right to condemn either of our parents. What they did thirty years ago has nothing to do with us. Cy and Leona have protected you from any public ridicule because of your father's mistakes, however much you question their motives. You have a cousin who has remained as loyal a brother as anyone could ask for. They all did what they thought was right out of love for you. The same way my parents did for me.

"I feel sorry for the loss you've suffered, for what all of you have suffered," she hurried to say before resolution failed her. "I know how much it hurts to feel responsible for damage to another person's life that can't be undone. I've stared at that painting for weeks now. At first, I saw only a face condemning me for what I did, but I finally decided to give the guilt over to it. I don't feel it anymore. I can forgive myself now and get on with the business of enjoying life. You've helped me do that, Cain. Now you have to help yourself."

She turned and walked to the door. Pausing a moment in the open portal, she looked back into the mute features of the man she loved.

"Don't throw your life away because of this tragedy," she said quietly. "You have too much to live for." A sad smile flitted across her lips. "Goodbye, Cain. I'm sorry that none of us has been perfect enough for you. Maybe you *can* only find that kind of perfection on a face in a painting."

CHAPTER TWELVE

"Hello, darling."

"*Mama*!" Uttering a cry of joy, Jade held out her arms to greet her parent. "What on earth are you doing here?"

The pale woman standing at her doorstep was the last person Jade would have expected to see. She'd spent last night wrestling with the sheets—and with her feelings. She'd barely dragged on a dressing gown and started her morning coffee when the doorbell sounded.

"Why didn't you tell me you were coming, *Mama*?" she asked as she guided her parent to the nearest chair. Kellus Hartman presented a more colorless image than Jade ever remembered seeing before. Her mother's silver hair was pulled back in its customary chignon, but the gray suit she wore and a complete absence of makeup seemed to add to her pallor. "I would have picked you up at the airport."

"Actually, I didn't know if you'd want to see me." The mother fixed searching eyes upon her child. "I suspect by now you know I've been less than honest with you?"

"I know now you *were* the woman in the painting," Jade offered in reply. "I know you were married to Louis Morgan at the time and that you and his brother had some kind of personal involvement that led to your husband's death. Cy and Leona Larkin told me about the cabin in the country where you and Del Morgan met sometimes. But I have a feeling I still don't know the complete truth about that tragedy." She studied her mother's pallid countenance. "Other things have happened since I talked to you on the phone. I tried all last evening to work up the courage to call you again. I need to know everything, *Mama*, if you're ready to tell me."

Kellus Hartman nodded. "I see now that I must. I've had to gather a lot of courage myself during these past few days. I knew you'd probably not given up on your quest to find out the truth, and it was likely you'd learned pieces of it already. I finally decided I had to talk to you face-to-face."

For seconds, two pairs of compelling green eyes locked on one another. "Would you like some coffee?" Jade asked, breaking the silence. "I just made a fresh pot."

"Yes, that would taste good," her mother said. She leaned back against the chair cushion and uttered a weary sigh. "I've had a very long journey." The statement seemed to hint at more than an exhausting airplane ride.

Jade served the coffee, and, for minutes, the two women sat in silence enjoying the stimulating beverage. Finally, Kellus Hartman put down her cup and began to speak.

"How much did Leona Larkin tell you about her stepbrother's death?" she asked in opening.

Jade offered a mute word of thanks that her mother had arrived just now. She vowed this time to seek out the whole truth, however much it hurt. To that end, she related briefly everything the Larkins had told her.

"Is that what Del's son has been told, as well?" Kellus asked then.

"More or less," Jade explained. "He hired a private detective to investigate. I'm sure the detective related the stories the police and the newspapers reported. What Leona told all of us was, of course, the information her stepbrother had shared with her."

"So Del's son is convinced his father murdered his uncle?" her mother surmised.

"Yes." Jade exhaled a long breath. "Cain has lived in dread of some horrible family secret for so long it devastated him when he found out it was true. My face—your face—in that painting, my pressing to find out the truth from the Larkins, it's all made him think I've been a party to some ongoing conspiracy against him. He won't listen, even to me anymore. I've lost him, *Mama*." Her voice broke as she spoke aloud the finish of her hopes.

"Oh, darling." Kellus Hartman reached out and took hold of her daughter's hands. "I've tried to save you from the kind of suffering I lived through. But now, it seems, vengeance has sought me out through you."

"Tell me what really happened, *Mama*," Jade said, swiping away a tear. "I have to know."

Her mother nodded and, seeming to feel she might not deserve physical reassurance from the child she had borne, she withdrew her hands and clasped them tightly in her lap.

"I'm not innocent," she began with a deep breath. "It's true I had a terrible marriage with Louis Morgan. He abused me verbally at first, then physically, as well. The further his business sank toward ruin, the more he took out his frustrations on me. And he always seemed so jealous of his brother. Del and I felt a kinship, partly, I suppose, because we'd both been treated so badly. Del tried to persuade me to divorce my husband, but my religious upbringing forbade it. Marriage was a sacred commitment until death parted us…" She winced when she spoke the final phrase.

"I encouraged Del to continue his painting," she went on after a moment's pause. "He had so much talent. Eventually, I agreed to pose for him. For awhile, our relationship was totally innocent, although I did keep it a secret from my husband. Del and I used to meet at his property outside of town. He'd bring his son along and we'd have picnics near that old cabin you spoke about. It wasn't long, though, before we realized our feelings had become more than just friendship. But we didn't give in to our physical need for each other…except that one time…" Again Jade saw pain in her mother's eyes as she recalled the memory.

"The boy had a cold that day so Del left him with his housekeeper and came alone to the cabin to meet me. As soon as he saw me, he knew I'd been crying. Louis had been very drunk the night before, and he'd convinced himself that I was to blame for his miserable life. When Del pressed me to tell him what had happened, I burst into tears all over again and admitted my husband had beat me. Del was so tender; he held me and kissed me, and I didn't have the strength to deny my feelings for him any longer. We made love, beautiful, passionate love. I knew then I would never love another man with the same passion. But I felt so guilty about the great sin we had committed, I told him I could never see him again."

"And yet you did see him again?" Jade prompted when her mother lapsed into wistful silence.

"Only one more time." As Kellus Hartman continued, her keen jade eyes seemed to see again a vision from decades past. "The day I followed Louis to the cabin."

"What did happen that day?" Jade asked.

"The men were already fighting each other when I arrived. I burst into the cabin and tried to pull them apart, but I must have seemed ridiculous. Louis had beaten me so badly that morning I could barely stand myself. It had taken what little strength I had left to make it to the car and drive out there. All I could do was watch while the two men hammered at one another. One look at my torn face seemed to give Del renewed strength. He fought like a wild man, and, eventually, he managed to overpower Louis and knock him unconscious. Then he tried to make me leave with him, but I couldn't do that. Regardless of what had happened, I still felt a duty to my marriage. I had to try one more time to reason with Louis. I finally convinced Del to go on alone after I promised to meet him later."

"Then your husband was still alive when Del left?" Jade solicited.

Her mother nodded. "Louis woke up minutes after Del drove off. He stalked out of the cabin, more insane with rage than before. He lashed out at me, of course, blaming me for everything. He struck me over and over until I was barely conscious. Then he dragged me back inside the cabin and set it on fire."

"He intended to leave you there?" Jade interrupted, horror-stricken by what she was hearing. "To burn along with the house?"

"Yes," her mother confirmed. "But the plan backfired on him. The oil stove in the cabin had been knocked over when the fight started. It exploded in Louis' face when he lit the first match. I had regained enough of my wits by then to crawl through the flames and make it outside. A passing truck driver saw the smoke and found me there."

"But Leona said…they all thought you'd died at the hospital. How did you manage to fake your death?"

"Your father, bless him, did that for me. When the truck driver got me to the hospital, I was barely alive. And I wanted to die. I tried to pull out all the tubes they had hooked up to my body. Your father came into the room in time to stop me. He asked me why. I told him the whole story, hoping he'd let me finish what I'd started. But he didn't. Instead, he believed me.

"He'd heard the news reports and we both knew that as soon as the police were permitted to question me, they'd conclude that Del and I had killed my husband together. The housekeeper had overheard Louis accuse me of adultery the morning it happened, and she'd already told the police about it. She'd named Del, of course, as the man my husband branded as my lover, and the police were certain they'd be able to locate and arrest him very soon. When I was strong enough to be moved, the police would have come for me, as well."

"But you were never arrested were you, *Mama*?"

"No, I wasn't. Your father saved my life again. He faked a death certificate and moved me to a private sanitarium. My face looked so different no one there connected me with the woman in the news. Jason paid for my care until I was well enough to leave the hospital. Then he took me home with him and began a series of surgeries to restore my features—not the way they were, of course. I could never be that woman again."

Jade felt her own troubles shrink beside the enormity of her mother's suffering. "I know you must have been grateful to *Papa*, but did you love him ever?" she had to ask.

"Of course I did, darling. Not with the same passion I'd felt for Del. But when I finally agreed to marry Jason, I loved him very much. He was aware by then that his heart condition would shorten his life and he'd given up his medical practice. Even with my features so changed from my old likeness, he knew I didn't feel safe living in America. So he bought the house in France and we started our life there shortly after you were born."

"Oh, *Mama*." Jade slid from her chair and embraced her mother. "How much you've endured. I had no idea."

Kellus Hartman's pale face beamed with a rush of color. "I thought you might hate me, *ma petite*," she choked out.

"Hate you?" Jade stared at her parent. "I only wish you'd told me this years ago so I could have shared your burden."

"I do, too," her mother said, dabbing at the wetness on her cheeks. "Now, about Del's son," she said, seeming to will back the strength to compose herself, "what will you do about him?"

"I don't know yet, *Mama*. I've told him I love him, regardless of anything he's learned about the past. I don't see what else I can do. He has to find his own strength to work through his feelings now."

"I wish I could help you mend things with him, darling." Kellus Hartman reached for her daughter's hands again and squeezed them to her breast. "I feel I've contributed to this breach between the two of you."

"No, *Mama*," Jade reassured her parent. "Actually, you've helped, just by coming to me when I really needed you. As for the other, well, Cain will have to do that himself."

"Just a few minutes, you can manage for that long," Jade told herself for the tenth time. Business meetings had whisked her over half the globe during the past few weeks, and jet lag had taken its toll on her energy. Arriving back in the U.S. only hours ago, she felt much too tired to attend a social gathering this evening. But Daniel had treated her with kindness. She owed him at least a token appearance at his engagement party.

The ballroom of the Empire Hotel where she'd stayed so many weeks ago was splendidly decorated with an autumn theme. The room was crowded with guests, a blessing, she thought. That would make it easier to come and go without attention.

She could have claimed a perfect excuse for avoiding this party. She'd been given no forewarning that she'd be included in the celebration. Only this afternoon when she'd been thumbing through the mail accumulated during her absence had she discovered Leona's invitation and a later note urging her to attend. Though she appreciated the Larkins' graciousness, it would have been so much easier to call in a few days and say she'd arrived home too late to make it.

All other reasons aside, she knew what had almost caused her to skip this gathering: Cain might make an appearance, and the last thing she wanted was a confrontation that was sure to reopen the wounds she'd sought diligently to heal during these past weeks. However, she'd already purchased a wedding gift for Daniel and his bride in the Orient, an exquisite wooden carving, so, in the end, she'd decided to risk abrief visit to deliver it.

As Jade had hoped, she was able to wander unrecognized among the celebrants (fortunately, the wide-brimmed hat she wore to complement her simple burgundy cocktail dress shadowed her most recognizable features). She had to marvel at the elegant affair Leona had put together on such short notice. Momentarily, she felt a pang of regret that circumstances denied her the option to remain and enjoy herself.

So far, she'd seen no sign of Cain. Nor had she seen or heard from him otherwise, not since that final encounter in the cottage. After days without a word, she'd finally accepted that their relationship was over. She recalled the phone conversation with Leona Larkin when she'd explained about her impending business trip. It hadn't taken long for Cain's foster mother to realize she was effectively saying goodbye for good.

******

"Will you be gone long?" Leona asked, initially registering surprise at Jade's disclosure about the company meetings overseas.

"At least two weeks, perhaps more," she told her friend.

"I hope you'll let us know when you'll be returning," Leona pressed. "We'll want to have you over for dinner."

Jade paused, trying to choose her words carefully. In the end, she sensed that nothing but outright candor would do. "I don't think I should come for dinner again, Leona. I think it would be less awkward for everyone if I just bowed out of your lives quietly."

A brief silence followed, then, "We're so sorry that all this happened," she said. "We never wanted it, you know."

"Of course, I know that," she was quick to say. "I'm sorry, too, that it has to be this way. I've felt very close to you."

"Oh, my dear, you've been like a daughter to us." Jade heard the break in Leona's voice as she spoke. "Won't you ever come back to us?"

"I'm sorry, Leona, I'm afraid I can't. Cain has made it clear how he feels, and I don't know how to change that."

"It breaks my heart that he can't see what a treasure he has in you." Leona was barely able to speak the words. "Please forgive us all."

When Jade replaced the telephone receiver, she felt a sense of loss so great her heart could hardly bear it. Why did it always cost so much to love?

Despite the strain it added to her already heavy heart, Jade realized that this business trip had provided her with the balm she'd needed to start her healing. Her boss's request that she be in Tokyo when the firm's executives arrived for conferences with their Japanese counterparts had allowed her a few days free which she used to accompany her mother home. The two women had enjoyed a renewed closeness after her parent's revelations about her own personal tragedies, and Jade had been anxious to see Kellus Hartman back to the small villa where she'd lived her safe existence for nearly a quarter of a century. When mother and daughter parted this time, both had gained new strength to continue with their lives.

And now after three weeks of almost constant meetings, Jade was back in Atlanta, exhausted in body, yet refreshed in spirit. She'd gained praise from all participants in the business discussions for her excellent command of languages. The pain of Cain's rejection would take time to heal. In the meantime, she was determined to get on with the business of living.

As she wove her way among the guests at the party, Jade counseled herself to simply be happy for Daniel. She would stay long enough to say hello to the Larkins, offer her gift and depart.

"What do you think about all of this?"

Astonishment spun her around. But the sound of that familiar male voice had already identified its owner.

"Cain! what—?"

"I said what do you think?" There again was that seductive eloquence which had dissolved her defenses so often in the past. "Do you approve of Leona's little soiree?"

He looked very much as he had on that first occasion when she'd found him so intimidating. He was dressed in a black tuxedo, perfectly fitted to accentuate his fetching masculine attributes. His appearance overall seemed in perfect form. Three weeks hadn't been nearly enough time to get over him, she thought dejectedly. As he moved closer, she saw one edge of his mouth curve into that look of suppressed humor which at former meetings had bandied her senses back and forth between seduction and annoyance.

Which was it now? She recalled his amusement at her naivete during their early encounters. Did he now find it comical that she hadn't been able to stay away from this family gathering?

Her senses cautioned her now that her only protection lay in distancing herself from him quickly. A confrontation with Cain this soon after its recent wounding only laid her heart open to more harm. The mere sight of him was already causing that member to lurch inside her breast like an engine with a damaged transmission.

"No," she reminded herself in a stern whisper, "I will not run. I promised myself I could handle this, and I will."

"I've always admired Leona's creative abilities," she spoke up before Cain could offer another remark to catch her off guard. "This lovely party merely reaffirms that she's a very loving mother."

"So you're enjoying yourself?" He'd stopped so close that their shoulders nearly touched. Heat seemed to emanate from his body straight into hers. Her muscles ached to move a little closer, to feel for a second the sear of his flesh against hers. She bit hard into her lower lip to quell the sexual need burning inside her. She mustn't permit any outward sign to show him the power he still had over her.

"May I get you some champagne?" he prompted. If he sensed her struggle for control of her senses, he didn't provide any signs of his own. "I can assure you it matches the excellence of everything else here." His eyes traveled over her in quick appraisal and he smiled appreciatively.

"No-no, thank you," she said, fighting the urge to step away from him before he dissolved her defenses entirely. "Nothing for me. I can't stay long. I'd hoped to offer Daniel and his fiancée my congratulations, though, and at least say hello to Cy and Leona before I leave."

Sucking in a deep breath, she steeled herself as she turned to face Cain squarely. In this up-close view, she noticed that something *was* different about his appearance. His eyes had lost their granite-coldness, but dark shadows, a classic indicator of loss of sleep, showed there now.

"I'm sure Leona's here somewhere," he said. "I just noticed her a few minutes ago giving some kind of instructions to one of the servers, always wanting to make everything perfect, you know how she is."

Jade nodded absently and glanced around the room. Why couldn't she spot one of the Larkins and end this torture?

"We can count on seeing you at Daniel's wedding, can't we?" Cain asked. Again he attached those dark eyes on her, seeming intent on reading her response. "I know everyone wants you to be there."

"No, I don't think so." She had to wonder why he seemed suddenly so interested in seeing her. Weeks ago, hadn't he slammed the door for good on her participation in his life? "I'm not much on weddings these days. I've pretty well given up on marriage for the time being."

"You don't mean that?" His reaction unshielded, he looked at her as if she'd just delivered the first blow to a stake through his heart.

"I do mean it," she pronounced stiffly. "Now, if you'll excuse me—"

"Why, Jade?" he interrupted. He looked even more wounded.

"Because love, marriage, a future together, everything our relationship promised, it was never going to happen." She returned his stare with a look of earnest resignation, hoping the set of her features would make him understand finally how much he'd thrown away. "I doubt if you ever did really love me. Your obsession with an ideal in a picture was what you were in love with. But I'm not a picture, Cain. I'm a real woman. I didn't materialize out of thin air to assume the form of a girl you dreamed. And what I felt for you was real. It makes me sad that you've let your obsessions destroy you—not just with the painting, but with the sins of your father, as well. I hope someday you'll realize that, and maybe then you'll be able to love a woman who's real, not just an ideal."

She thought he might argue with her. Instead, he asked quietly, "Why did you come here tonight, Jade?"

"I-I don't know," she said, fumbling for words as fatigue chipped away at her control. She wasn't nearly ready for this confrontation. She had to get away from Cain. "I couldn't just ignore your mother's invitation. Your family has been very kind to me. And I'm happy for Daniel. Mostly I came, I guess, because I wanted to see at least one wonderful thing come out of all of this."

"One thing wonderful has come out of it, Jade." The strain she'd seen before in his features relaxed away like a tortured prisoner who'd just gained hope for a reprieve. "More than one thing."

She allowed her gaze to drift into his for a moment, trying to comprehend his meaning. Then she blinked her senses back to reality.

"Tell Daniel I stopped by, will you," she said, pushing the gift she'd brought into his hand. "And say hello to Cy and Leona for me."

As she turned away, Cain's free hand snaked out to lock onto her wrist. "You're not leaving me?" Why did his words sound more like a pronouncement than a question? Hadn't he been the one to end their relationship?

"I told you I can't stay," she said, steeling her heart against the warmth of his touch. "I've had a very long and tiring day and I really don't feel like partying."

"Then I'll take you home. I haven't had a chance to talk to you yet."

"I have my car. Besides, we have nothing more to talk about, Cain."

"Leave the car," he said, as if he hadn't heard her dismissal. "I'll have someone pick it up for you."

Gently but firmly she reached out and removed his fingers from around her wrist.

"No, Cain. No." A moment later she turned and faded into the crowd.

"Oh, Cain, she's not leaving, is she?" Leona's agitated question distracted him from watching Jade disappear out the door.

"I'm afraid she is," he said, handing Jade's gift over to her. He felt a lot of the same emotion his foster mother must be feeling. He had to thank whatever forces in the universe that had brought Jade here tonight. He'd racked his brain lately for a way to approach her after her return from Tokyo. In the end, he'd urged Leona to write an appeal to her in a personal note to follow the party invitation. How much they all missed her, the family would be so disappointed if she didn't join them, that sort of thing. Jade's appearance had convinced him of one thing—she hadn't erased him from her life completely yet.

Nevertheless, he hadn't managed to persuade her to stay and talk to him.

"I'd hoped you might talk her into staying awhile," Leona said like an echo. "You don't think this is the last we'll see of her, do you?"

"Dear God, I hope not," Cain said almost in a whisper.

He had only himself to blame if he'd used up all his chances with Jade. When he'd finally regained his senses enough to try to salve the wounds he'd inflicted upon her, Leona had let him know she was gone. Unable to accept his foster mother's conviction that it was more than a business trip out of the country but a final farewell to the whole family, he'd waited weeks for her to return. Finally, he'd called her office, only to learn that the meetings in Tokyo had run longer than originally planned, and Jade wasn't expected back for at least one more week.

With hope fading that she'd make it home in time to receive the news about Daniel's engagement party, he'd felt it flicker anew when he'd spotted her in the crowd tonight. (That face of hers, so indelibly imprinted on his senses, couldn't escape his notice, even with much of it shadowed by her hat) As travel worn as she must have been, she'd looked so good to him, he'd wanted to dash over to her and wrap her in his arms. When she had greeted him with such coldness, he'd nearly blurted out a plea for forgiveness on the spot. In the end, though, he'd accepted that neither response would gain him anything at the moment. So he'd let it drop and endured the torture of watching her walk away from him again.

"What are you going to do now, Cain?" Leona asked, the worry in her tone more profound than ever. "You won't just let her go, will you?"

"I'm going to talk to her again," he said.

"But what if she won't see you?"

"She'll see me, I'll make her see me," he pronounced with renewed conviction.

So far, Jade had managed to stave off her weariness by sheer force of will. Now, however, she felt that force beginning to falter as she fumbled inside her purse for her valet ticket. Handing it to the nearest attendant, she waited impatiently while he brought her car around.

More than a long plane ride had reduced her to this state of total exhaustion, she realized with the drifting of her thoughts. Her desperate struggle to maintain control during the past several minutes had consumed what little energy she had left. But she'd made it through the encounter with her ex-lover and held on to her composure. If the fates were kind, she'd never have to see him again.

The valet rewarded with a generous tip, she slipped behind the wheel of her car and breathed out a sigh of relief. Tossing her hat onto the seat beside her, she combed trembling fingers through her long tresses. Just a few more miles and she'd be home in her own bed, she thought, fortifying her lungs with one last cooling draught of night air.

Then she put the car in gear and started out of the parking area. The engine didn't sound right, though, and she'd barely made it onto the side street before it began to lose power and then died altogether.

"No, oh, no, please don't do this to me now," she begged, praying that the engine would restart.

After several tries, though, she had to accept that it was no use. She was stuck.

Frustrated to the point of tears, she yanked the key out of the ignition and looked back toward the parking area. No one in sight. Where were the attendants when you really needed one? Well, she'd just have to help herself, that's all there was to it. Locating her cell phone, she was about to dial the number for roadside assistance when the sound of a male voice stopped her.

"Jade, I thought that was you."

"Daniel!" she sang out, surprised apprehension dissolving into a sigh. She rolled down the car window and smiled up at Cain's brother. "How wonderful to see you again. Why aren't you at your party?"

"Why aren't you?" he volleyed back, returning her smile. "Or are you just arriving?"

"Oh, Daniel, no, I've already been inside, but I could only stay a few minutes." she said apologetically. "I just got back from Tokyo and I'm beat. I was trying to leave but something seems to be wrong with my car. The engine just died on me."

"Pop open your hood and let's take a look," he suggested. "It could be the battery. Do you have jumper cables with you?"

"Sure." While Daniel checked under the hood, she found the cables. "Here they are," she said, handing them to him.

"Get in and try to start the engine again," he said minutes later when he had the cables hooked up to both their cars.

"Still nothing," she said disappointedly, when after several minutes, the engine refused to start up again.

"Well, nothing seems to be loose in here," he said after several more minutes of checking under the hood. "Tell you what," he said brightly, "I'll drive you home and we can call a professional to look at this."

"Oh, Daniel, you will not," she responded in immediate protest. "Everyone's waiting for you at the party. I'm sure the auto club will send a tow truck in a few minutes. I'll be fine."

"I'm not about you leave you stranded on a public street," he countered. And before she could offer more argument, he went on to explain, "Everyone knows I won't be back for awhile. Some friends had to leave the party early so I took them to the airport. It's not that far to your apartment. They can spare me a few more minutes to take a lady home." Responding to her continued look of skepticism, "Please, Jade," he said, "let me do this for you, even if it's just to say goodbye properly."

The message behind his final plea was clear. He felt he should have done more to heal the breach between her and Cain. He was a good brother; it wasn't his fault that things couldn't work out.

"All right, Daniel, and thanks," she said wearily. Grabbing her hat and purse, she climbed out of her car and allowed him to guide her to his Mercedes. His steadying arm felt so good to lean on, she admitted silently when he handed her into the passenger seat.

"Why did you really leave the party so soon?" he asked when they'd left the side street and were moving onto the freeway. "Did you get to meet Georgette? I know shewas anxious to become acquainted with you."

"I wanted to meet her, too," she said with another long sigh. "And to visit with all of you a few minutes. But I ran into Cain and..."

One silvery brow lifted. "Oh, I see. So things never got straightened out between you two?"

"How could they? He never tried to call me before I left for Tokyo. His silence all these weeks has made it clear our relationship is over. I'd accepted that, but I'd hoped I wouldn't have to face him tonight. But no such luck; he spotted me right away."

"Are you still in love with him?" He glanced her way, searching her eyes. "Is that why you left town so abruptly?"

She offered a dispirited nod. "He's made his choice, though. I can't change what is. I'll just have to try to get over it. But I can't think about that tonight. Tonight I'm not up to making sense of anything. I just want to go home and get some sleep."

Daniel reached over and patted her hand. "Sure, Jade. I'm sorry. I wish I could have done more to help."

She managed a wan smile. "You did all you could, Daniel. You're a good and loyal brother. Cain doesn't know how lucky he is to have you."

She leaned back against the fine leather seat, sucked more cool air into her lungs and tried to push away the gathering mist of fatigue—and her thoughts of Cain.

"Let's talk about you, Daniel," she said as they drove. "Why aren't you having this engagement party in Quebec? I was puzzled when Leona's invitation said you were celebrating here in town. I thought by now you would have returned to join your fiancee and her family for this party."

"I had planned to go right after you left the country, but unfinished business kept me here longer. Georgette has been very patient." He smiled over at her. "You two are much alike. She understood why I couldn't leave just now so she flew here to join me. Mother came up with the idea to organize this engagement party for us. Georgette's family has another one planned for us when we return to Quebec." He laughed. "By the time we're done, we'll have had so many ceremonies we'll have to live happily ever after."

Jade smiled, trying not to envy Daniel and his bride. But for circumstances, she and Cain might be enjoying similar ceremonies. "Well, I'm happy for both of you," she said through a yawn. "I hope you'll apologize to Georgette for missing your party and give her my best wishes. And tell her, also," she said, stifling another yawn, "that I'm glad her knight in shining armor happened by in time to help this damsel in distress."

"About that, Jade," he returned hesitantly, "I want to tell you—"

She swallowed another yawn. "Can you tell me later, Daniel? I'm afraid I'm too tired right now to listen."

"Sure, Jade." He patted her hand again and turned his attention to his driving. Making no further effort to press for conversation, he maneuvered the luxury automobile through the gathering traffic.

Jade lolled her head against the headrest, unaware that her profusion of red-gold hair spilled enchantingly over her shoulders. Briefly, her mind attempted to speculate about Daniel's unfinished remark. Then her eyelids fluttered closed, and blessed oblivion washed over her troubled spirit.

CHAPTER THIRTEEN

"No! No, you mustn't stop me! I have to get to him!"

"Jade! Jade, wake up!"

Cain? Jade's fuzzy brain questioned. Her eyelids fluttered in a vain struggle to remain in that whimsical world where Cain had called out to her.

"Jade, you're dreaming. Wake up."

Through the shadow of her eyelashes, she tried to make out the face that belonged to the voice. "Cain?"

Dark eyes stared back at her. They looked as tired as before, though not as haunted. "Good morning," the voice said.

Like a raw recruit startled by the sound of reveille, Jade jerked to attention. "Cain, where did you come from? Where's Daniel?"

She sat bolt upright, realizing at once she was not in Daniel's automobile, but in someone's bed. Her eyes darted wildly about the room. Its elegant dark wood furnishings suggested a man's bedroom. Suddenly, her gaze came to a crashing halt as it collided with her own body. Where was the dress she'd been wearing? In fact, except for her black silk camisole and panties, she was completely naked!

"What is this?" she demanded. "Where am I?"

A lazy smile crawled onto the lips of the man seated on the edge of the bed next to her. "Well, let's see if I can answer all your questions. I'm here because this is my house and this is my room. Daniel's downstairs having breakfast with his fiancee and the rest of the family. So, obviously you're home, where you belong."

"Why did Daniel bring me here?" she persisted, trying desperately to sort out the events after she'd gotten into Daniel Larkin's car. "He was supposed to take me home."

Wild thoughts raced through her mind. Could Daniel have betrayed her this way? She'd been so tired...Could she have remained unconscious through her own kidnapping? Had she slept in Cain's bed—with Cain? Reflexive humiliation smacked her cheeks with hot color.

At once, she willed her logical mind to hold her emotions in check. Cain was already finding this too amusing. Peeling back the covers, she swung her feet onto the floor and gazed around the room for her clothes. But the room was in perfect order.

"Where are the rest of my things?" she asked. When he didn't answer, "You and your brother must have had a great time undressing me and putting me in your bed," she flung accusingly at her captor. "What was I, the door prize for his bachelor party? Funny, I thought Daniel was my friend." She made another quick perusal of the room, this time to decide which door led to a closet.

"Daniel *is* your friend," Cain spoke up. At least, he had the decency to look a little chagrined. "He had no part in this except to drive you here. When he handed you over to me, you were sound asleep, but still fully dressed, I assure you. I'm the only one who's touched you. I asked my brother to try to convince you to come here to talk to me. But when you fell asleep, he decided to let me convince you myself. His only transgression was bringing you here without your consent. And, believe me, he didn't feel very good about tricking you."

Cain had risen along with her as she exited the bed, but he didn't try to stop her when she headed for the double doors at the opposite end of the room.

"Then why? Why would Daniel do such a thing to me?" Speaking as much to herself as to Cain, she busied her hands with flinging open closet doors. "It's easy enough to figure out this little drama you cooked up between you. You and Daniel must have arranged a signal when I turned down your offer of a lift home. Before I could get to my car, he must have paid the attendant to cripple the engine, then waited to 'rescue' me. All that brotherly sympathy," she scoffed, "it was just part of the charade."

When her searching revealed no sign of her clothing, she turned to face Cain with a renewed verbal attack. "Cain, enough of this! You can't keep me here. Give me my clothes!"

"Relax, I'll get them for you in a few minutes," he said in that remorseless tone she remembered from previous occasions when he'd intended to thwart her efforts to defy him. Well, not this time!

She stood with her back against the closet door, arms folded across her breasts, and looked squarely at him. "Why are you doing this?" she asked quietly.

He shrugged. "I told you, this is where you belong. When you wouldn't let me drive you home, I knew you were still too upset with me to listen." Before she could reply to that, he held up a defending palm. "I know, I know, you have good reason to be angry with me. But now that I have you here, I can't let you leave until I've had a chance to make you listen."

Her already unsteady control skidded dangerously near the edge. She had to swallow hard to hold on to it. Make her listen? To what? What new fixation had taken control of Cain? Had he mixed her up completely with a woman in a painting?

"You had every chance in the world to speak to me weeks ago," she reminded him. "I wasn't hiding from you."

"I know that, but I wasn't thinking straight back then."

She shook her head disbelievingly. "And now you *are* thinking straight?"

"For the first time in years, yes, I am," he answered levelly.

What should she do? she wondered. She wasn't really afraid of him. In fact, underneath her anger and frustration she felt even sadder for him now. Apparently, he had convinced himself that he could somehow regain the ideal he'd manufactured in his mind if he held her here long enough. Surely, though, his family hadn't realized what he planned when they participated in this scheme.

"All right, give me my clothes and we'll talk," she said in an attempt to humor him.

He shook his head. "Not just yet. You're still angry and you might walk out on me before I can convince you of anything. I can't risk that, not now." He took a step toward her, but when she raised her palms against him, he stopped.

"Cain, this is madness," she said, quickly sifting her brain for possible options to save herself (she could think of no easy ones). "How long do you think you can keep me me here?"

He made an appreciative inspection of her scantily clad body. "Dressed like that, I'd say as long as I want."

She'd guessed right; he did think he could recreate his perfect image of her. His family's presence in the house was what he was counting on to hold her. The bedroom door probably wasn't even locked. He'd merely disposed of her clothes, and now he counted on her modesty to keep her hostage in this little prison. He hadn't thought this through quite well enough, though. He'd forgotten that the naive, vulnerable girl of those early days had steadily faded away during recent months, and a capable, independent woman had replaced her.

"I suppose I'll just have to find a maid who understands these things," she offered defiantly and started toward a door she hoped would lead to the hallway.

"I've asked the maid to work downstairs so we wouldn't be disturbed," he said to checkmate. Even so, she noted a hint of shock in his voice. "You'll find the family in the breakfast room," he said with renewed confidence. "I'm sure they'll be glad to see you." His chuckle indicated he believed he'd recovered the upper hand. "But I'm afraid you're going to have to meet them just as you are."

Jade leaned her head against the doorjamb for a moment and prayed for one more spurt of strength. She'd bluffed her way this far; she had to carry through if she really wanted to save herself from Cain Delancy. He'd manipulated her life for months. She had to break free once and for all. Even if she had to pay with her pride to do it.

"Well, if that's the price," she murmured hoarsely and jerked open the door.

"Jade, no!" He slammed his palm against the door, jarring it shut. The next second, he caught her by the shoulders and turned her into his embrace. "Oh, Lord, no!" he said, shaking his head vehemently.

As much as she'd ached to have his arms around her again, she managed to hold her body rigid. She bit painfully into her lower lip to keep from sobbing out her humiliation. However, no amount of willpower could hold back the gush of silent tears transforming her eyes into liquid jade before spilling onto her cheeks.

"God, I never meant it to come to this," husked from Cain's lips. "I'm sorry, I'm sorry…" He swallowed when his voice broke. As if sapped of energy, his arms dropped from around her and he stepped away. "Your clothes are hanging in the bathroom." He nodded in the direction of the only door she'd left untried. "Through there."

Jade didn't look at him. Head held high in one last effort to salvage her pride, she slipped past him to the bathroom and closed the door.

Prostrated by the pain in his chest where his heart had been yanked out, Cain slumped onto the bed. He'd gone too far with this mad scheme to win Jade back. He'd expected surprise, even anger, at his actions. But, ultimately, he'd get her to listen while he explained how wrong he'd been to doubt her and begged her forgiveness. And she would forgive him, he'd been so sure of it he'd even convinced his family to help him.

However, while he'd been wallowing in his own self-pity, he hadn't really noticed how Jade had changed. Generous-spirited and loving always, nonetheless, she now possessed an intensity of will which enabled her to override her sensual inclinations when her pride was at stake. So confident about the outcome of his plan, he hadn't considered that she might view his actions as merely an attempt to degrade her. And that was something she could never forgive.

"God in Heaven, what have I done!" he gritted in despair. Now when he'd finally commenced repairing his imperfect life, he'd destroyed the one thing that had always been perfect. Overcome by emotion, he dropped his head into his hands and wept.

Jade found the rest of her clothing, along with several feminine toiletries, neatly laid out in the dressing area of the large bathroom. She washed her face and completed a hasty toilette before she dressed and brushed her hair.

Suddenly, she realized the only way out was past Cain. She didn't think she could hold out against another confrontation; her control was in tatters as it was. She could only hope Cain had regained his senses enough not to hinder her escape this time.

She need not have worried. Cain sat stock-still on the edge of the bed. His head was bowed, and his fingers clenched tightly behind his neck like a passenger going down in a doomed airplane. He didn't even look up when she emerged from the bathroom and hurried past him toward the door.

She had her hand on the doorknob when something inside her cut short her escape. She couldn't leave him like this. Regardless of the reckless way he'd shown it, he needed her. His compulsion to hold onto her at cross purposes with his torture about the past, he'd been driven to this desperate act. Although she doubted he would ever be able to reconcile the two enough to make a commitment to her, she still cared about him. She removed her hand from the doorknob and walked back to the bed to sit next to Cain.

At once, his head shot up. His eyes glistened like polished walnut, and even a quick swipe across his cheeks with the heel of his hand couldn't keep her from noticing their wetness.

"I thought you'd gone," he got out in a husky whisper.

Apprehension disappeared beneath the deluge of affection that poured from Jade's heart at that moment. She reached out and touched his cheek. "I couldn't leave you like this," she said gently. "I love you."

With a whimpering sigh, he reached out his arms and pulled her to him. This time, quite apart from resisting, she wrapped her own arms around his waist and clung to him. She offered her lips and he took them in a kiss as tender and worshipful as those he'd delivered during their first mating.

"Oh, Jade, I've messed up everything royally this time," he murmured against her lips. "I'm sorry, so sorry."

"Talk to me," she said after they'd fortified themselves with several more kisses.

"I went to visit my father," he said in opening.

Her eyes widened and she pulled slightly away so she could search his face.

"Your father? You mean—?"

He nodded. "Delancy Morgan."

"But how did you find him?"

"Cy and Leona managed through his lawyer to arrange a meeting. I imagine Leona told you that Lawrence Collier has acted as the family's go-between all these years. The professor has been a good friend to my father, as well as to the Larkins, so I have to forgive him for his part in keeping this secret. Anyway, all of them got together to launch an appeal on my behalf." He reached to touch her cheek. "Not that I deserved it after the way I treated all of you."

She closed her hand over his. "That's all behind us now. Go on."

"After you left me, I brooded for days over what I'd found out. Daniel was the one who finally brought me to my senses. Brother or not, he said, he wasn't about to feel sorry for a man who was fool enough to push you out of his life.

"How right he was," Cain said, squeezing her hand. "I knew it, too, as soon as you disappeared out the door. I was just too stubborn to admit it."

"So, tell me about this meeting with your father," she prompted. The way he'd behaved at their last meeting, she was surprised he'd been willing to face Delancy Morgan. "Was Daniel also the one who convinced you to see him?"

Cain nodded. "Daniel didn't pull any punches that day. He made me see that I didn't know nearly all the truth yet. He said I didn't have any right to judge my father until I'd heard his side of the story. He'd been just as diligent as Cy and Leona have in trying to arrange a meeting between the two of us."

"I know. Daniel told me. Cain, they weren't conspiring. They were all just trying to help—just as I was."

"I don't know why I couldn't believe anyone cared about me," he owned regretfully. "Especially you.

"Anyway," he continued after a moment of silence, "a meeting was finally set up with my father in Paris." When she showed surprise again, "Yes," he affirmed, "Paris. Another ironic twist, I know, but that's where he's been living all these years, a nobody surviving in the back streets of the city. He has a small apartment over a bakery which he he seldom leaves, I understand. But when I visited Paris on business a few years ago, Lawrence got word to him that I'd be there and the name of my hotel. He said he came every day and watched me coming in and out of my hotel, yet he never approached me."

"What torture that must have been for him," Jade spoke up in reflexive sympathy. "Would you have recognized him, though, if he'd passed you on the street?"

Cain shook his head sadly. "He and I share some of the same features, I'm told, but it was hard to see. He's only sixty years old, Jade, but he looks much older. Every day of his suffering is engraved in his features. He was a great artist, a genius, you've seen his work. But can you guess how he makes a living? He paints faces on little figurines for sale in gift shops."

She held tightly to Cain's hand for a moment, sharing his feelings. "Did it help to talk to him?" she asked finally.

"I think so. In fact, I think it helped both of us. My father seemed to take it as a kind of forgiveness that I wanted to see him. That's all he wanted from me, Jade, just to know I forgive him."

"And could you forgive him?"

Cain nodded. "After seeing him, I realized he'd paid for what he did. There are no iron bars around him, but he's been a prisoner all these years just the same."

"Did he tell you what happened that day at the cabin?"

He nodded again and, during the next few minutes, related virtually the same story Leona had told her.

"Now," she said when he'd finished, "I want to tell you what really happened that day."

His brow lifted in puzzlement. Then realization appeared in his features. "Your mother—?"

"Yes, my mother told me, the day after we last spoke. She'd traveled all the way here to Atlanta to explain the truth to me. I didn't mention it to Leona before I left for Tokyo, partly because I wanted *Mama* to be settled back at home before anyone knew she'd come to the States. And too, the way things were between us then, I doubted that it would matter." Regret showed in Cain features and she patted his hand in reassurance. "I thought after I came home I'd write her a note asking her to let me know if she ever heard from your father. Now you can tell him the truth yourself."

Cain was suddenly very alert. "Tell him what truth?"

"That he wasn't to blame for the death of his brother. It was an accident. And he should know, too, that the woman in the portrait, the woman he loved, is still alive. She's my mother, just as you suspected."

While Cain listened with rapt attention, Jade related the events her mother had explained, including what had happened after Delancy Morgan left her that day at the cabin.

His visage etched with dismay, Cain shook his head over and over. "My God, why did he run? Why didn't he stay and defend himself?"

"You must know the answer to that, Cain."

"Yes, I guess I do. If he'd stayed, my father would probably have been convicted of murder. And your mother, as well. Adulterous lovers, that's most likely how the court would have viewed them, conspiring to kill the husband who stood between them. In any case, the scandal would have gone on for years. He tried to spare me all that."

She nodded. "Then you can't doubt any longer that he loves you—just as Cy and Leona do."

Cain's brow creased into another look of regret. "It seems I've been wrong about everybody. I know now that my foster parents told me the truth; they didn't have a choice about adopting me. My father explained that he was grateful to them for taking me in, but he just couldn't let them take me away completely. I think he always hoped he'd be able to return for me someday.

"What I hope is that my foster family can forgive me one day for doubting them. And you, Jade," he added, looking earnestly into her eyes, "I hope you can forgive me for the things I said and thought about your mother—and about you."

"I'm sure your family has already forgiven you," she said softly. "I know I have."

He didn't answer. He merely looked away, as if he needed a minute before he trusted himself to speak again.

"Your father won't go back on his agreement with Cy and Leona because of all this, will he?" she asked, partly to help Cain past this emotional hurdle.

"No," he cleared his throat, "no, he won't. He knows the Larkins kept their word. I told him that seeking him out was all my idea."

Jade nodded. "I'm glad. They've worked hard to build their business. They deserve to keep it."

"Yes, they do." A smile edged onto Cain's lips, one that said all the dark shadows had been pushed away. "It's little enough payment for putting up with me all these years."

"You haven't been all that hard to take," Jade said, a grin forming on her own lips. She held onto Cain's hand for a minute, yet neither of them seemed to know what else to say. Unable to terminate the awkwardness any other way, she got up from her place beside him and picked up her things. "You want to tell me where my car wound up?" she asked. "I should get home."

That brought him to life. He shot up from the bed with the desperate urgency of a drowning diver seeking fresh air.

"You can't leave!" burst from his lips.

"Oh, Cain," she said in exasperation, "not again. This is where we started, remember? Surely, you're not still thinking you can keep me here?"

"But now that you know—"

"What do I know? That you understand now that you never had anything to be ashamed of? You never did, anyway. Remember me, I'm the woman who would have married you no matter what your father was."

"And you won't marry me now?" He looked as if his very life depended on her answer. "But, Jade, you have to marry me—now today, if you want. I can't lose you again, I need you."

Realizing from the way Cain spoke that he was finally willing to commit to her, Jade felt her heart leap; nevertheless, she struggled to keep her telling features mute. After all he'd put her through, he deserved a little uncertainty.

"I don't *have* to do anything of the sort," she said. "Besides, I don't remember ever receiving a proper proposal of marriage from you, just a lot of reasons why you couldn't marry me. The last thing I do remember is being made a prisoner by you and your brother and you trying to manipulate me yet again. That doesn't sound like the actions of a man who has changed. It sounds like a man who wants things his own way—just like before."

"But I didn't mean to-I had to have a chance to-I had to persuade you to change your mind." His expression blinked back and forth between guilty frustration and desperate supplication.

"Change my mind about what?" Though she'd removed some of the severity from her tone, she kept her features unyielding.

"About leaving me?"

"I didn't leave you. You pushed me away."

His expression elevated to one of guarded hope. "What can I do to pull you back to me? Don't I have a chance?"

"Maybe. If you really are finished with all those dark thoughts you've harbored for so long. And you're ready to accept my love exactly as I offer it—unconditionally."

Her tone had mellowed completely now, but the look she gave him said *her* life depended on what he answered.

"I swear it on the honor of both my families." As he spoke the oath, his gaze never wavered from the probing scrutiny of her green eyes.

Jade nodded and stepped closer. Then she curled her arms around his neck and settled into her cherished place against his body. "Then ask me," she whispered.

The murmur of, "Thank God," echoed through a shaky sigh a moment before his arms came around her. "I love you, Jade," he said, swallowing to steady his voice before he asked, "Will you marry me?"

"I love you, too," she answered in a firm, certain voice. "And yes, I'll marry you."

Their kiss started out gentle, then deepened slowly until passion became its driving force. Mixed in with it, however, was the complete trust that comes with shared commitment.

Long since graduated from the shy novice who knew nothing about lovemaking, Jade reveled in her power to arouse her partner. Her senses enveloped by passion, she barely felt it when Cain eased her backward onto the bed. With no fears to restrict her, she matched his eagerness to surrender completely to their sexual appetites. Clothing quickly became a frustrating impediment to their ultimate closeness.

"If you'd just left well enough alone a few minutes ago, I wouldn't have this problem," Cain growled, his shaking fingers struggling to unfasten her zipper.

"Haven't I told you before, you worry too much instead of asking for help?" she teased. Then with amazing thrift of motion, she wriggled free of her undergarments.

"I'll remember that from now on," he murmured, his attention focused on the glory of her naked body. She felt him shudder with sexual anticipation when she moved against him to undo his zipper.

"To hell with this!" Unable to stand it any longer, he sprang off the bed and literally tore off his clothing. "I want all of you touching all of me—now!

"You are the most magnificent creature I've ever seen," he said, his voice heavy with increasing passion. His fingers glided over the velvet softness of her naked flesh, delivering more silent praise.

What the two had learned during past months about the pleasuring of one another was launched into practice. In a heady mix of desire and worship, they engorged their senses with the touching of one another. When this tantalizing activity no longer satisfied their need, they joined their bodies in the ultimate sensual pleasure. Heated senses flamed higher and higher until, with one last shattering explosion, they burned out their passions.

"God, I've missed you," husked from Cain's parted lips. He rolled slightly away and gathered her close. "I was dying without you," he added in a muffled whisper against her hair.

"I thought I'd lost you," Jade told him in an equally hushed tone. "I love you so much."

His brow pinched slightly. "Oh, honey, can you really forgive me for being such a coward?"

She reached up and stroked his cheek. "Of course, I can. I've wasted a lot of precious time myself brooding over events I couldn't help—with Bonn. It's funny, even though I knew that painting wasn't me, at the same time, I began to realize I was letting it heal me gradually of the guilt I'd suffered from all those months."

He nodded. "I'm glad."

A gap of silence made her remember where they were. Realization forced out a nervous chuckle. "Maybe we should get dressed and go downstairs," she ventured. "What will your family think about our staying up here so long?" The heat scorching her cheeks reminded her she still had a few inhibitions that pushed in at inconvenient times.

"They'll think exactly what they should think," he answered without a trace of repression, "that I'm trying my darnedest to show the woman I love how much I want her to become part of my family."

My family, Jade mused in silent thankfulness. All the shadows *had* faded from her lover's eyes. He knew now that he'd always been surrounded by love—from both his father and his foster family.

"So you don't think we should put in an appearance for breakfast?" she teased.

"Are you hungry?" he fished.

Her feelings now as unashamedly naked as her body, she laced her fingers at the back of his neck and pulled him to her. "You can't tell? And I thought I had such an expressive face."

He pursed his lips and scrutinized her features with sensual appreciation. "Yep." he said a second before his mouth covered hers, "you definitely look ravenous to me!"

EPILOGUE

"Do you think we're doing the right thing, sweetheart?"

Jade looked up at the man she loved. "I hope so, darling," she answered thoughtfully.

A casual onlooker might have considered this a strange scene: With everything in place for a wedding ceremony, the bride stood at the steps of the altar holding the train of her white satin gown while she spoke in hushed whispers to the groom. However, anyone acquainted with the situation knew this was the couple's second trip to the altar.

Married only days ago in a quaint little chapel in Atlanta, they had made arrangements for a European honeymoon. But first, they had to fulfill a very important commitment at this other small chapel outside of Paris. In a few minutes, Mr. and Mrs. Cain Delancy would repeat their vows a second time for the benefit of just two people—Jade's mother and Cain's father.

Neither of these two guests knew the other would be in attendance at this special ceremony. That bit of information which the couple had withheld from their respective parents was the reason for their current misgivings.

Both Kellus Hartman and Delancy Morgan did know, of course, that the other was alive. (The ultimate irony in a situation riddled with it, the two had lived within a hundred miles of one another all these years.) Cain had revealed to his father, also, the complete truth about the death of Louis Morgan and Kellus' ultimate escape. As soon as a second discreet meeting could be arranged with him, the couple had flown to Paris with a two-fold purpose: to clear the air with truth and to get to know one another's parents.

When he saw Jade for the first time, Delancy Morgan had looked for a moment as if he might collapse. But after he'd recovered from the initial shock and accepted that she was not Kellus, but her daughter, he'd received her with a warmth of feeling that elevated almost to worship. His parting words had convinced her that he viewed her marriage to his son as a compensation of sorts for the love he had lost.

Cain's first meeting with Jade's mother might have proven awkward in a different way. He didn't remember her from his childhood. Despite his having come to terms with his past, still, Jade had feared he might view Kellus Hartman merely as the woman responsible for separating him from his father. Certainly, the Cain of a few weeks ago, confused, tormented, unable to accept love, might have behaved with cool politeness at best.

But Jade need not have worried. This new Cain, who now accepted that love meant understanding and forgiveness and a wealth of other unselfish emotions, had not hesitated to reach out to her mother.

"Thank you for giving me Jade," he'd said, when he embraced the woman whose portrait had opened the way to restoring his life.

The pale face of Kellus Hartman seemed to radiate with renewed luster today as she sat alone in a pew near the front of the chapel. Her brilliant green eyes beamed with pride at her daughter and new son-in-law. Delancy Morgan hadn't appeared, but his son had already confided that his father might prefer to observe from the shadows.

"Here we go, darling," Cain spoke up, alerting Jade. Dressed in a morning suit and smartly groomed, as usual, he looked as handsome as he had when he'd pledged his life to her a few days earlier. "Meet me at the end of the way?" he solicited in a whisper when his lips brushed those of his beautiful bride.

"You can count on it, my love," she whispered back. "Forever."

Cain paused for a moment just to gaze at his bride. Those red-gold tresses fashioned into a crown of curls on top of her head and woven through with tiny flowers gleamed like morning sunshine. She looked so beautiful, she seemed almost unreal. But she was real, as real as the love she'd lavished on him these past weeks. As real as the love she'd taught him to give in return. He felt his body tighten with delicious anticipation of all the nights of love they had yet to share.

He hoped, even as he knew she did, that they could gift their parents with some small measure of the same happiness.

The organist commenced the prelude and Cain stepped to his place at the altar. When he looked toward the rear of the chapel, he expected to see his bride beginning her march down the aisle toward him. Instead, she'd paused for some reason at the entryway. She held out her hand now and a man stepped forward and took it.

Dressed in a dark suit and tie, Delancy Morgan still looked old beyond his years. Nevertheless, his demeanor, too, had gained new vibrancy during recent days. A smile brightening his features, he offered his arm to the winsome bride and escorted her to the altar. When he placed her hand into that of her handsome groom, his smile grew wider, wiping away more years from his countenance. Nodding to his son, he stepped back and turned to face the woman who'd won his own heart so many years ago.

"Kellus, it is you," he said, holding out both his arms in supplication.

The fragile woman rose slowly from her pew. For long seconds, she stood and stared with those compelling jade eyes. Then she stepped forward into the arms of the man she'd never ceased to love.

"Del," she said in a breathless whisper, "it's been so long."

"Yes, beloved, so very long," he returned in a husky whisper a second before his lips touched hers.

The bride and groom, forgotten for the moment in the midst of this heartwarming reunion, smiled at their parents, then at one another.

"They'll be all right now, won't they?" Jade said.

"Yes, my darling, I think we all will." Cain raised the delicate hand of his bride to his lips and pressed a kiss into her palm. Then he turned to the priest and announced in a firm, sure tone, "We're ready to begin."